A PROPOSAL TO SECURE HIS VENGEANCE

A PROPOSAL TO SECURE HIS VENGEANCE

KATE WALKER

MILLS & BOON

First published in Great Britain 2018
by Mills & Boon, an imprint of HarperCollins*Publishers*
1 London Bridge Street, London, SE1 9GF

Large Print edition 2018

ISBN: 978-0-263-07380-5

MIX
Paper from
responsible sources
FSC® C007454

This book is produced from independently certified FSC™ paper to ensure responsible forest management. For more information visit www.harpercollins.co.uk/green.

Printed and bound in Great Britain
by CPI Group (UK) Ltd, Croydon, CR0 4YY

For dear Kathy W, one of the special friends
I've gained from Writers' Holiday—
even if you only come there in July!

CHAPTER ONE

THE WALK DOWN the aisle on your wedding day was supposed to be the longest walk in the world, and today it certainly felt as if that would be the case.

Imogen shivered at the way the words whirled in her head as she contemplated the stone-flagged aisle of the small village church, making her admit to the state of mind she'd been trying so hard to hide—even from herself—for the past few weeks.

A feeling that had grown so much worse as the date of her wedding had come closer, so that now it was just a couple of days away and she still wasn't ready at all.

She doubted if she would ever be ready.

It could all have been so much worse. She could have had no one to turn to, no one who could help her and her family out of the morass of disaster they had fallen into, and with it the loss of the stud that had been in the family for over a century. Even perhaps the prospect of a prison sentence for her father.

No one to push her into a marriage she didn't want but saw as the only way she and her family could possibly go forward.

Imogen pushed her hands through the tumble of black hair that fell onto her shoulders, exerting extra pressure with her fingers as if she could erase the chaos of her thoughts.

It was the only way, she told herself silently. Adnan at least was a friend; they liked each other—always had—and they both had so much to lose if this didn't go ahead.

Besides, there was another possible advantage, she hoped, that perhaps, after her marriage, the scandal press would let go of the hateful nickname they used whenever she or her sister Ciara were mentioned. If this redeemed Ciara's reputation too, left her free to go forward in life and put her own shadows behind her, then that was another reason it would be worth it.

She'd always loved this little village church.

The church where her parents had married, where she'd been christened, and her sister after her. She had so loved being an older sister, until their mother had run away with a new, much younger lover, taking Ciara with her. At least the preparations for this wedding had brought Ciara back to the family home where she belonged and now, hopefully, could actually stay.

After a lifetime apart, she had only discovered the whereabouts of her sister a couple of years ago, but the two of them hadn't had any real time to get to know each other properly. Ciara since then had been living and working in Australia, and Imogen's whole attention had had to be focused on fighting to save the reputation and financial position of the stud. But she'd adored Ciara from the moment they'd met again and if she could do anything to help make up for the loss of happiness and family life that Ciara had endured, then she'd do her damnedest to make sure that happened.

She owed Adnan so much. After all, it could have been someone else she was so deeply indebted to, someone else she was having to marry.

Someone like Raoul Cardini, a wicked, tormenting little voice whispered into her subconscious.

'No!'

Involuntarily she started away from the pew beside which she had been standing, the surge of memories taking the strength from her legs. She was so distracted that she didn't hear the heavy wooden door open behind her, the soft footsteps on the floor that marked the arrival of someone else into the church.

He hadn't expected to see her here, Raoul reflected as he stood just inside the open porch, staring down the aisle at the tall, slender figure who stood with her back to him, one hand on the polished edge of the pew beside her. Just seeing her like this, so unexpectedly, brought all the bitterness, the cold fury that he'd been fighting to hold in check bubbling up inside him.

The original idea had been to wait until the pre-wedding dinner tonight to implement his plan for revenge. He had been looking forward to seeing the sudden rush of shock in her eyes, the way her expression would change. Yes, he was sure she would fight to keep control, do everything she could not to show how she was feeling. She was good at that, he recalled, remembering the cool control he had seen her exhibit at times during the two weeks they had spent almost every moment in each other's company.

She certainly hadn't shown any emotion when she had left him, two years before, her face tight and controlled. He hadn't begun to suspect the secrets that lay behind that expression, the truth she had hidden from him without a qualm. She'd never even revealed a hint of that life-changing secret until it was gone, the tiny beginnings of what might have been his son or daughter thrown away with the help of the expensive clinic she'd taken herself to. He'd never seen her composure break.

Except for the night she and her sister had been caught by the paparazzi emerging from the casino arm in arm, he recalled, his hands clenching into fists at his side. Neither of them had seemed in the least bit steady on the towering heels they'd worn.

The Scandalous O'Sullivan Sisters! the headline above the photo had shrieked, and it had been in that moment that Raoul had put Imogen and Ciara together, realising that the surname of the nanny who had threatened to ruin his sister's marriage was shared by the woman who had destroyed his chances of being a father. He had recognised her in a moment, but had been stunned to see both of them out of control in a way he had never seen the older O'Sullivan girl before.

Except in bed.

Raoul felt a curse echo inside his thoughts as he fought the rush of heat through his body. He'd thought he'd wiped that particular memory from his mind but it seemed that all it needed was her presence, just metres away from where he stood, and every cell was inflamed. He couldn't afford to let that distract him from his purpose.

She looked a little different, but he knew inside she would be the same. Still tall and elegant, but now with a glossy mane of black hair tumbling down her back. It was longer than before. He remembered the crisp, silky feel of the sharp pixie cut she'd sported back then, the smooth strands catching the gleam of the sun. She was dressed differently too, in a plain white tee-shirt and tight-fitting jeans, simpler and more subdued than the bright skirts and sundresses she'd worn on the beaches at Calvi or Bonifacio. She'd grown thinner too, the tight-fitting denim clinging to shapely hips and long, slender legs, the occasional stylish rip in the material exposing the pale cream of her beautiful skin. She didn't look like a woman who had carried a child. But then, of course, she had never let her baby live long enough to change the shape of her body, had she? It had barely existed before it was gone.

It was shocking how even that dark knowledge didn't stop his more basic male urges responding to the feminine appeal of her.

No! She would not remember Raoul!

Imogen shook her head sharply, desperate to drive away the last lingering threads of memories that bruised her soul; memories she had never wanted to recall. But it seemed that just dredging up that once-loved name from the silt in which she'd hoped to have buried it brought everything rushing back.

'The longest walk in the world.'

The voice spoke suddenly from behind her, its rich, husky accent obvious on the words. An accent that sounded alien in this small Irish village. But not unknown. She knew that voice only too well…but how she wished she didn't.

'Is that not what they say?'

'I— No…'

She whirled around to face the newcomer, spinning so hard that she went over on one ankle, needing to reach out and grab a nearby pew for support. But it wasn't the worn, polished wood that her fingers closed over. Instead she felt the warmth of skin, the strength of muscle and bone under her grasp, and there was the scent of lemon and bergamot in her nostrils, blended with a sensual trace of clean, musky male skin.

It was a scent that jolted her sharply out of the present and right back to a holiday in Corsica two years before. A starlit night, still warm after the burning heat of the day. The slide of soft sand under her feet, the sound of waves breaking in her ear and the hard, warm palm of the man who had just become her very first lover tight against her own as they walked along the beach.

The man who, just six days later, had broken her heart.

'No?'

That shockingly familiar voice was back, softly questioning in her ear, and she blinked hard against the red mist that had hazed her eyes.

This had to be a mistake; a crazy, mindless fantasy. Her unwanted memories had created a mirage in her mind, conjuring up an image of the man she had weakly let into her thoughts for a moment but now wanted so desperately to forget.

'R-Raoul…'

The name stumbled from her lips as she forced herself to focus and found it only made matters worse. That tall, lean frame was a powerful, dark force in the silent atmosphere of the little church.

'*Ma chère* Imogen.'

It was soft, almost gentle. But that gentleness was a lie, she knew. There was no tenderness in this man, as she should have realised from the start. If she had, she might have escaped with her body and her heart intact. Her baby might never have been conceived—or was that actually the worst thing that could have happened? To have known Raoul's child growing inside her for even the shortest time had brought her such joy, such happiness, that she could never have wished it hadn't happened. Even if it had ended so cruelly.

'I'm not your *chère* anything!' she retorted, pulling away from him with a force that rammed her hip into the wooden side of the pew. 'Not now—not ever! And I never wanted to be.'

'Of course not.' His tone made a mockery of her declaration.

He moved slightly, stepping out of the direct light and into a spot where the multi-coloured gleam of the sun burning through the stained-glass windows turned his face into a mosaic of blues and reds, a tiny touch of gold gilding the hard slash of carved cheekbones. The skin was drawn rather more tightly across those bones than it had been before and there were a few more lines around his eyes than she recalled but, if anything, those tiny signs of the passing of years only added to the devastating appeal of his stunning features. The colours from the window played like a kaleidoscope over the white shirt he wore, sleeves rolled up over long, muscular forearms. The shadowy interior of the church hid the burnished glow of golden skin, softly hazed with crisp black hair, but Imogen didn't need to see to remember.

She knew what those arms looked like when gilded by the Corsican sun; knew only too well the feel of them curled around her waist, pressed close up against her skin where it was exposed by the vivid blue bikini she'd felt brave enough to wear in the heat of the sun. And in the heat of his appreciative eyes. She knew what it felt like to lie with her cheek resting on the strength and solidity of his bones, the power of his muscles, the scent of his skin in her nostrils as the beat of her heart slowly ebbed and she slipped into sleep, exhausted after a night of love-making.

She knew too well—and she didn't want to remember.

'You'll forgive me if I don't believe that,' he drawled now.

'Believe it! It's the truth.'

The burn in her veins chilled as she watched his beautiful mouth twist in a cynical response.

'That wasn't what you said at the time.'

It sounded almost gentle, but the ice in his golden-eyed stare warned her she'd be a fool to believe there was anything kind in him at all.

'What I said at the time didn't mean a thing.'

Imogen drew in her breath in a rush, fighting for control. She felt she was being dragged backwards into her past, swallowed up by a dangerous quicksand, suffocating slowly and painfully. Head over heels and crazy in love, all she'd done was to say that she didn't want their sun-filled idyll to end, that she wanted to stay with him. She'd never expected he would turn on her, accuse her of being a greedy gold-digger and dismiss her—for good, he had declared.

'Those were the foolish, thoughtless declarations of a naïve adolescent. I'd had too much sun, too much wine…or something.'

Too much of Raoul Cardini, certainly. But she'd never been drunk when she was with him—she'd never needed to be. He was intoxicating enough to make her mind swim in heated abandon. She'd never had a head for wine anyway, or the taste for it. Except for that one crazy evening she'd spent with Ciara just after they'd rediscovered each other. They'd both been struggling with the darkness that had fallen over their lives, and as a result the joy of the evening together had gone to their heads faster than the most potent alcohol.

'None of it was true—none of it was real.'

'And none of it is relevant now.'

Cold and cutting, it made her feel as if the ground beneath her had shifted disturbingly. She'd known two years ago that he could turn away from her without a second's thought, dismissing all she'd believed they'd been to each other in between one breath and another. But she'd never heard him state it in words of pure ice that he tossed in her face without a blink. And once she knew just how impossible she had found it to forget him, that realisation slashed deep into her soul.

She wished she could find the strength to turn and walk right out of here. Brush straight past him and head for the door. The trouble was that she didn't think 'brush' would be the word to describe the way she would encounter Raoul on the way. Even whispering past the tall, forceful body of the man before her would be like thudding straight into a brick wall.

'Nothing between us is *relevant* at all. So, if you'd just let me past…'

An elegant wave of his hand indicated the fact that there was plenty of space for her to walk by him.

'Be my guest.'

She was nearly past him when he stirred slightly and she could hear the hateful smile in his voice as it drifted after her.

'I'll see you back at the house.'

It stopped her dead, her head ringing as if his words had been a blow.

'I think not!'

It was only now she realised, shockingly and disturbingly, that there was a question she had never asked. One that should have been right at the forefront of her mind from the moment he had first spoken to her but she'd been too stunned even to consider. She'd never thought fate could be so unkind. It was bad enough that he should be here, now, so close to her wedding day, but to think that this was not just an appalling error of chance…

'You're not coming back to the house!'

'Oh, but I am.'

That brought her spinning round, needing to see his face. The deadly smile was still there in his voice but there wasn't a trace of it in his expression.

'No way. I mean…why are you here at all?'

There it was. The question she should have asked from the start. The one that, she now realised, she hadn't dared to ask because she'd feared the answer.

Now the smile was not just in his eyes but very definitely curling the edges of that obscenely sexy mouth. At least, it was obscene for Imogen to consider *anything* about this man sexy. That was what had caught her in the first place, trapping her in the coils of his dark sensuality, taking her life out of her hands and putting it into his, to torment and break as he wished.

'Your father invited me, of course.'

The deadly nonchalance with which he tossed the words at her made her stomach tighten.

'Dad? You're kidding!'

That was just too much. She actually laughed in a blend of shock and relief, at the realisation that this simply could not be true. How could he ever be here for the wedding? How could he have been invited when no one but her knew him well enough to offer him an invitation? She sure as hell had never let anyone know that for a brief space of time he had once been such an important part of her life. Her short-lived summer love affair and its bitter consequences would neither have concerned nor interested her father.

'Do I look as if I'm joking?'

He looked supremely confident, totally at ease, and with not a trace of amusement on his carved features.

'My father would never invite you here. And definitely not for this wedding.'

'Why not?'

There was the flash of challenge in those golden eyes now, clashing with the disbelief in her own stare.

'Not good enough, is that it? You think, *ma belle*, your father would not want to invite a simple olive farmer to his daughter's wedding of the year?'

'Oh, come on!'

She had to cover up her reaction to that casual '*ma belle*', needing to hide the way it had the bite of acid. Once she had loved to hear him call her that, had gloried in a new-found sense of feeling beautiful in his eyes. But now the bitter memory of how quickly she had gone from being *ma belle* to a mere nothing, a plaything tossed aside and abandoned on the beach where they had first met, curdled in her stomach.

'We both know you're no simple olive farmer and you never were.'

That had been the pretence he had hidden behind when they'd met. He'd let her believe he was a hard-working farmer who was delighted to meet this young Englishwoman on holiday and spend time with her. His friend Rosalie had been the one to warn her that there was more to Raoul Cardini than that. But even she had never revealed the full story. It was only when Imogen had got home and, still nursing the hurt in her heart, had been unable to resist looking up the beautiful island of Corsica on the Internet that she had found the truth that had rubbed salt deep into the wounds his rejection had inflicted on her.

'I don't think the Cardini olive oil empire could ever be described as just farming!'

What had she said? It was only the truth, after all, but it was as if she had flung some vile insult into his face so that his head went back, bronze eyes narrowing, beautiful mouth clamping tight, turning his lips into a hard, thin line.

'Not just the olive oil empire,' he said. 'At least get your facts right.'

'Of course there's more, isn't there? More you didn't trouble to tell me. Did you think it wasn't worth me bothering my head about?'

She flicked her eyes at him, there and away again fast, wanting him to see that she really couldn't give a damn about anything else he hadn't revealed to her. At one time, discovering the fact that, like her family, he was a dedicated breeder of fine horses might have brought them together. But the time to care about the lies he had told, the secrets he had kept from her, was long gone. The memory of the one secret *she* had kept from him burned in her soul, threatening to destroy her if she let it free.

'Your father thinks it is. That's why he agreed to a deal I proposed. And he wanted to mix business with pleasure.'

Could he make that last word sound any more toxic? She knew something was very wrong—it had to be. How could her father have agreed to a business deal when there was nothing left of the family business? If there had been any other possibility then she wouldn't be here, living through her last days of freedom before she walked down this aisle with Adnan Al Makthabi. The marriage was supposed to save the Blacklands Stud from complete ruin. It was supposed to ensure they didn't have to sell off the few remaining horses, including the magnificent stallion Blackjack.

The cost of the stallion had crippled their already overly strained finances, the loan her father had insisted on taking out to pay for him depleting further an already empty bank account and adding thousands to the interest repayments.

But at least Adnan and his family wanted Blackjack—perhaps more than they wanted Imogen herself.

'He suggested I come now and share in the celebrations. And he offered me a room in Blackland House for the week so we could discuss the deal at the same time.'

He made it sound perfectly reasonable, natural even, but the nasty twisting sensation in Imogen's stomach told her it couldn't possibly be that way. Her father couldn't discuss any sort of 'deal'—he had nothing to offer! From the date of her wedding, he wouldn't even own the stud—or Blackjack.

'So tell me—what did you use to buy my father's interest?'

She'd gone too far with that. Dangerously so. She could see it in the way a muscle ticked in his cheek, the glare that had turned the warm colour of his eyes to ice in the space of a heartbeat.

'I don't buy my business partners. Ask your father. *You* might not want me here but, believe me, your father does. He invited me to stay and be a guest at your wedding—so, naturally I said yes. I wanted be here to watch you plight your troth to your perfect bridegroom.'

Raoul spat the words at her before he spun on his heel and marched away, down the aisle and out of the church. The staccato sound of his angry footsteps echoed through the silent interior of the church until the heavy wooden door slammed loudly behind him.

CHAPTER TWO

THE SUN WAS burning away the fine dawn mist that had clouded the distant hillsides as Imogen turned the bay mare and reluctantly headed back to the stud. The long, solitary gallop on her favourite horse had been a welcome time of peace and quiet in the bustle of the weekend. Time to reflect and draw breath before considering what her next move might be where Raoul Cardini was concerned.

Because of course Raoul was the real problem she had. The preparations for the wedding were well in hand, everything would have been fine if it hadn't been for Raoul's unexpected arrival and the crazy scheme that her father had embarked on to bring him here.

'Oh, why now!' she exclaimed aloud, making the mare's ears prick in response to the sound as they trotted down the path that led to the stables.

But she knew why. Adnan had revealed last night at the pre-wedding dinner that her father had mentioned Raoul's approach, his interest in the stud services and the stallion Blackjack in particular. But they had agreed to wait until the wedding was over, he said. Or that had been the original plan.

It was obviously not what Raoul believed, Imogen reflected now, slowing the mare to a walk as her hooves rang on the cobbled stones of the stable yard. Last night she'd finally managed to get the truth out of her father, discovering to her horror that things were as bad as she'd thought. Her father had planned to get the deal for stud services for Blackjack signed and sealed before the magnificent horse became the property of the Al Makthabi stud—which he would on the day of her marriage. Adnan had agreed to clear her father's debts, save Blacklands from destruction and restore it to something of its former glory, but only on condition that Blackjack became his as part of the deal.

If she couldn't get her father to cancel the whole thing then the wedding would be off. And even if she could she would still have to worry that Raoul would reveal everything to Adnan.

If that was everything. The mare danced sideways and whickered a protest at the way Imogen's grip had suddenly tightened on the reins.

'Sorry, Angel!'

She gave the sleek bay neck a reassuring pat as she struggled with the bleakness of her thoughts. Just remembering how Raoul had appeared at the dinner last night, dark and sleek in immaculate evening dress, made her throat close up. This was the man she had once thought of as her future, only to have that hope thrown back in her face. She couldn't believe he was here only to discuss a business deal with her father, so she was forced to wonder just what other wicked schemes were brewing behind that cold-blooded, heartless facade of his.

Last night she had thought all she had to do was speak to her father, demand that he break off this ridiculous deal with Raoul. It was only later, when she had had time to think about things, she'd realised how that might not solve matters. Instead, it might be like knocking down the first domino in a carefully planned and balanced arrangement, sending them all tumbling in a wild cascade. One that had the potential to destroy everything she and Adnan had worked and planned for.

'Almost there.'

The memory of the words Adnan had directed at her, the smile that had accompanied his statement, swirled in her mind as it had done all through the night.

She knew he had meant it as a reassuring smile. The trouble was that it had done nothing to soothe the jittery pins and needles that had been running through her veins ever since she had got back from the church.

Last night should have marked the moment when she and Adnan perhaps could have started to relax. They were, as Adnan had said, almost there. Last night's dinner marked the final stage in the preparations for the wedding. The day after tomorrow would be the main event and then after that, as man and wife, they could start to put back together all the pieces of the two families, the two studs, that had broken apart.

Instead, she now felt as if she was deeper into the mire of trouble than ever before—and it was all because of this one man.

'*Bonjour*, Mademoiselle O'Sullivan!'

The voice hailed Imogen as she dismounted from her horse and she bit back a groan of despair. This early in the day, she had hoped to have the fields and the stables all to herself, but of course she should have remembered that Raoul too was an early riser. So often when in Corsica he had stirred before dawn broke and was out before the heat of the day could start to build up. She had deluded herself at the time that as a farmer he had needed to tend to his land, never suspecting that he was up and out to deal with major business decisions so that he could return to the quiet hotel to share breakfast and then the rest of the day with her.

'Good morning, Monsieur Cardini,' she forced herself to respond, finding it hard to make it sound casual and relaxed, and failing miserably on both counts. 'I trust you slept well.'

'I was perfectly comfortable,' Raoul told her, crossing the yard to smooth a hand down the mare's soft nose. He watched the way Imogen's crystal-blue gaze flicked up once towards his face, then away again as soon as her eyes collided with his. 'But I should be no concern of yours. It was your father who invited me.'

'You are one of my wedding guests.'

That cool control was back, at least on the surface, but there was a tremor in her voice that pleased him.

'And I thought you would want to be at breakfast by now.'

'You know me.' Raoul watched her face as he spoke. He knew she was struggling to make polite conversation, but he had no intention of offering her any sort of lifeline. 'A cup of coffee is all I need to set me up for the day.'

She had once been inclined to chide him about that, he remembered, taking him out to one of the bustling little cafés in Ajaccio where she would attempt to entice him to eat something more.

'You work on the land,' she'd reproved. 'You need to eat.'

He recalled that she'd been almost addicted to the local bread made with chestnut flour and pine nuts, her appetite much better then than it seemed to be these days.

He'd watched her at dinner last night and if she had eaten any of the meal in front of her then he was a complete fool, Raoul told himself. She had stirred her food around, occasionally lifting her fork towards her mouth in a way that might convince anyone else, but not him. So totally aware of her as he was, there was no way he could have missed the fact that her fork had nothing on it.

Her sister was not much better, he acknowledged, having noted how Ciara O'Sullivan's eyes had barely left her sister and her fiancé, her own plate totally abandoned after one or two mouthfuls.

'I need to give Angel a brush down,' Imogen said, turning to lead the horse into her stall. It was obvious she wished he'd leave her alone, but Raoul had no trouble ignoring the blatant hint, strolling along beside her, one hand on the mare's flank.

He was seeing yet another side of Imogen O'Sullivan this morning. One which couldn't be more different from the elegant creature at dinner last night. Today she was dressed for riding, the simple white shirt and skin-tight jodhpurs clinging to her slender frame, her feet pushed into muddy black boots. Last night she had looked stunning and sleek as he had never seen her before, her burgundy silk gown glowing richly against the creamy pallor of her skin. The dress had had a deep, plunging neckline but one where her modesty was carefully preserved by the panel of delicate lace that had covered the lush curves of her breasts.

He couldn't see them, but he could remember. For a moment Raoul was totally distracted by the memory of the time he had undone Imogen's bikini top to expose the pure whiteness of her flesh where she had been protected from the sun, in contrast to the lightly tanned colour of the rest of her skin. Her breasts had been smaller then, each one just fitting into the curve of his palm. He had loved to smooth and caress them, tease the soft pink of her nipples into thrusting life. But just the thought of what might have made her breasts become larger had him biting down hard on his tongue to hold back the curse of rage that almost escaped him.

'So how are you liking your first time in Ireland?'

Imogen had obviously accepted that he wasn't going to leave her and had turned again to making polite, if rather forced, conversation.

'This is not my first visit here.'

There was an odd note in the reply, she recognised. One that warned of unexpected darkness at the bottom of what was just a simple statement.

'It's not? Was that recently?'

Her training at boarding school, the strict discipline of the nuns and their determination to turn out 'young ladies', stood her in good stead. She found that the disciplined part of her personality was working on auto-pilot while all the time, hidden inside, a far less controlled version of Imogen was stirring, uncurling, as if awakening from a long sleep and demanding a new sort of attention.

It reminded her of how it had once felt to be young and carefree, lost on the dangerous seas of her first sexually passionate relationship, the recognition of just how it could be between a man and a woman.

She still felt that way; even last night, with Adnan beside her and his ring on her finger. Adnan was the only man who could stand next to Raoul and match him, inch for inch in height, in the lean strength of his body, the force of his personality. Both were black-haired and brilliant-eyed—but, where Raoul's eyes were that gleaming, golden bronze, Adnan's were a cool, clear blue.

Adnan was stunning—hadn't the reaction of her own sister, when Ciara had first met her fiancé, left no room for doubts on that score? But it was Raoul who had knocked Imogen for six from the start, and now apparently had only to reappear in her life to make her feel as if the world had rocked dangerously and couldn't be righted again.

Raoul was nodding in response to her question.

'I was last here just over a year ago.' There was a dark note in his voice that tugged on already raw nerves. 'That was what first sparked my interest in your father's stud.'

It was only when Angel pushed an impatient nose into the small of her back, urging her forward, that Imogen realised she had stood stock still in confusion at the thought. Raoul had been here a year ago—when she and Adnan had just been starting to discuss the possibility of their marriage, of uniting the two families…

'And of course the magnificent Blackjack.'

Was that comment as loaded as he made it sound? The truth she knew about the stallion, and the way it made her father's deal with Raoul null and void, sat like a lump of lead in Imogen's stomach, forcing her to fight against a twisting rush of nausea.

Raoul reached forward and took Angel's reins from her limp hands, leading the mare into the open stall. The movement meant that their fingers touched just for a moment, something like electricity fizzing between them, so that Imogen couldn't stop herself from snatching her hand away as if she'd been burned. Angel didn't like the unexpected movement and shifted restlessly with a whinny of protest.

'Sorry, sweetheart…' she soothed, and the softness of her tone caught on an image in Raoul's mind, pouring acid onto an already bitter memory.

She had once spoken to him like that, in the darkness of the night, turning the sound of his name into a caress. The change that the spontaneous smile brought to her face was almost magical. Her eyes lit from within for a moment and her skin glowed. He cursed inwardly as the clutch of physical hunger grabbed at him right between his legs so that he shifted uncomfortably where he stood. Wanting to hide the betraying response, he bent to unfasten the girth and ease the saddle from the mare's back. He had never expected still to have this primitive and instantaneous response to her. Not after all he now knew about her. But it seemed that he could hate and hunger in the same heartbeat.

'Everyone's interested in Blackjack,' Imogen said and, although her eyes were on the bridle she was removing from Angel's head, he could tell that the words were not the throwaway remark she wanted them to sound like.

She wore no make-up, and the pallor of her porcelain skin was emphasised by the brush of dark shadow under those sapphire eyes, making them look faintly bruised and disturbingly wounded. She was thinner than when he had known her before, he thought again. He knew that brides were traditionally said to lose their appetites before the wedding, but she looked more like someone who was going to face execution rather than marry the man of her dreams.

But, of course, he wasn't the man of her dreams. Just the thought twisted harshly in his guts. If he'd even suspected that she really cared for Adnan Al Makthabi, then there was no way he would be here. But it was obvious this was a union arranged because of the financial benefits it brought—to the O'Sullivan family at least.

Once again, the cold-blooded gold-digger who had aimed to win herself part of his fortune was setting her sights on someone who had the money she sought. Someone who, it seemed, was more easily persuaded. Or so he'd believed. But, now that he'd met Adnan Al Makthabi, he wouldn't have put the other man down as the sort to be so easily fooled. He'd also been startled to find that he actually liked him.

But then yesterday he had discovered more about this proposed marriage than either she or her lying father had been prepared to acknowledge.

'Look, about…' Imogen began, then hesitated, broke off and, when she began again, Raoul was sure that she had not taken up where she'd left off but had veered onto another topic altogether.

'Where did you get to last night?'

She tossed the question at Raoul, trying so very hard to make it sound casual and relaxed, and failing miserably on both counts.

'Nowhere.'

'But I saw you leave…'

The words faded awkwardly and he raised a dark, cynical eyebrow as he saw the moment she realised she had given herself away. She should have been occupied with her guests, her family and friends, but she hadn't missed the fact that he had left the dinner early, with no explanation.

'I needed some air.'

He had been suffocating in the atmosphere in

the room. Three O'Sullivans—because of course the father had been there, knocking back the vintage champagne as if it were water—was more than enough for anyone to take. Not caring if anyone noticed, he'd slid his plate away from him, pushed back his chair and stood up.

The huge patio doors had been open to the garden, voile curtains wafting in the gentle breeze. He'd slipped out into the cool of the evening air, the silence of the night. Over to the left were the stables and the exercise yard, the occasional sound of the thoroughbred horses shifting in their stalls and whickering softly to each other reaching him across the stillness.

He could fall in love with this place, he'd admitted to himself as he'd strolled to the edge of the huge patio. The soft green hills and lush fields of this country were so unlike the rougher, drier terrain of his homeland. Here, the climate was closer to the one in the mountains—and of course there was always so much rain. It had been drizzling just a little and he'd held his face up to the moisture while drawing in deep breaths of the clear night air, filling his lungs with it and wishing he could fill his mind in the same way, to wipe away the anger and disgust he felt at finding himself amongst the members of this corrupt, immoral family.

He had almost left then, headed straight for the airport, onto a plane and away. Only the thought that if he went then the O'Sullivan family—the weak, corrupt father and those scandalous O'Sullivan sisters—would all get away with what they'd done and go on their way so carelessly had stopped him. He'd come here to make sure that didn't happen, and he was not going to back out now.

'I had hoped that you might show me around,' he said now, lifting the saddle and carrying it out of the stall to place it with all the other tack at the end of the stables. 'I'd like to see more of the stud.'

'I'm afraid I'm much too busy.'

Imogen flashed a cold, tight smile in Raoul's direction. She certainly didn't want to spend any time with him if she could possibly help it, and luckily the preparations for the wedding gave her the perfect excuse. He didn't need to know that there was nothing she had to prepare; that Geraldine Al Makthabi had everything in hand and that her future mother-in-law was enjoying every minute of the time she spent making sure everything was perfect.

'I have things to do. I am getting married…'

She flung the words at him like a dart. His presence might put her totally on edge, as if she was balancing on a very high, very tight rope with savage, bone-shattering rocks beneath, but she wanted him to understand that she was not alone and defenceless. She was in her family home, with her father and her sister—her fiancé just ten minutes away.

No…the instant curdling in her stomach at that thought brought a wave of nausea up into her throat. Adnan might be her friend, and currently her family's saviour, but he was also a proud and powerful man. His bloodline was saturated with the ferocious strength and arrogance of his Bedouin ancestors. She knew Adnan could be a hard man, a difficult man if his temper was roused. She'd heard stories of his reputation with women, and as a shrewd businessman, but she'd never had that side of him shown to her, and she never wanted to either.

He might have agreed to this marriage of convenience, but if it turned out to be anything else or, heaven help her, became *inconvenient*, then she had little doubt he would call the whole thing off without even blinking.

'I'm aware of that.'

Raoul's wickedly knowing smile left her only too aware of the fact that her attempt at attack had simply bounced off the cold steel of his armoured heart—if it really was a heart that beat inside that powerful chest.

'That is why I'm here.'

That—and what else? The words were on the tip of her tongue, but at that moment the door opened and Ciara wandered into the stables. Her red-gold hair tumbled round her shoulders, her green-and-white floral sun dress with its thin straps and flirty short skirt looking cool and comfortable in the already growing heat of the day.

'Hello, honey!'

Imogen's smile of welcome was blended with a

rush of relief at the thought that she was no longer alone with Raoul. The verbal fencing, neither of them coming right out and saying anything real, had stretched her nerves to breaking point. So much so that her heart was racing, her breathing shallow at the ordeal of just being in his company.

She was no longer the wide-eyed innocent who had first met Raoul Cardini on a warm summer evening on a beautiful Corsican beach. Met and fallen in love in the time between the sun burning directly overhead in the middle of the day, and the moment when that fiery ball had slipped below the horizon. She'd found herself in the warm darkness with her heart no longer inside her body but handed over to the care of the devastating man she had secretly nicknamed the Corsican Bandit.

If she had only known how appropriate that nickname would come to be, she would have turned and run, as far and as fast as she possibly could. But now she was two years older, she'd been tested by life, been down some long, dark tunnels and had reached the other side. Perhaps she was still bruised and bloody, with scars barely healing over deep wounds she'd endured, but she *was* standing, and she wasn't going to let anyone knock her down again.

But there was a huge difference between feeling that and actually challenging someone like Raoul Cardini to come right out and say exactly what his plans were. Especially when she didn't know how much danger her whole family was in.

She was aware of the way Ciara had reacted last night when she'd learned that Raoul was their guest, staying at Blacklands for the days leading up to the wedding. She had been subdued all through the evening and this morning; something was clearly upsetting her sister. She looked distracted and unusually unsure of herself, her eyes slightly puffy from lack of sleep in a way that concerned Imogen.

'*Bonjour*, Mademoiselle O'Sullivan,' Raoul inserted smoothly, strolling out of the tack room with lazy grace. Ciara shot a swift, strangely nervous glance in his direction.

'Morning,' she muttered almost inaudibly, her

hazel eyes focused on Imogen's face. 'So, what do we have left to do today, Immi?'

'Perhaps you can give me a guided tour of the stud that Imogen is apparently too busy to manage today,' Raoul put in, something in his lazy drawl scraping uncomfortably over nerves that were far too close to the surface of Imogen's skin. And Ciara's too, it seemed.

It was definitely an appeal for help that Ciara turned on her now—a plea to be rescued from heaven knew what—but it obviously had something to do with Raoul Cardini. Just what had frightened her sister so badly? Could it be that Raoul had come here not just for the business deal he had described, but perhaps for something to do with Ciara's past? Perhaps to do with the reason her job as a nanny had ended so rapidly, which her sister had refused to reveal to her? Imogen wished she'd had more time to get to know Ciara properly before the threat of total ruin had brought this wedding on them.

'There's plenty still to do,' she managed over-breezily. 'We have to sort out that hemline on your bridesmaid's dress…'

Imogen had made the right move. Immediately some of the tension left her sister's face and she almost smiled.

'And you promised Geraldine you'd help her with the name cards for the table.'

Raoul would never know just what a fiction that one was. Adnan's mother was totally in charge of every preparation for the reception and she would give anyone who tried to intervene very short shrift indeed. But the glance of gratitude from Ciara made the lie worthwhile. Her sister was already turning towards the door, looking like a rabbit that had just been released from a trap,

'I hope you have a good day, Mr Cardini,' Imogen tossed in his direction, not quite having the nerve to meet his stony glare, though she hoped her rather breathless tone could be taken for airy and unconcerned. 'I'll ask one of the grooms to give you the tour, if you like.'

The tour of the part of the business they'd be happy to show him, and not the one he'd obviously been angling for. The one that wouldn't let him pry into secrets that were none of his business. So far they'd managed to hide just how bad things were; she didn't want Raoul finding out more.

'Oh, don't bother.'

That lazy voice was back but she could catch the thread of steel that ran through it like a warning rumble of thunder before a storm broke.

'I'm sure I can manage on my own. You can find out the things you most want to know that way.'

It was meant to sound casual, indifferent, but there was so much more in his voice. The growing storm was coming nearer, dangerously so. She would have to find out just what was happening with Ciara and figure out how she could proceed from there. And she'd have to make sure that, whatever Raoul had in mind, he didn't get a chance to put it into action.

This sleek, elegant man with the closely cropped black hair, the burning golden eyes above lean, bronzed cheeks and the arrogant tilt to his proud head was so very different from the man she had met on that magical holiday. The young, carefree, raw and sexy Raoul with the suntanned skin, bare feet and over-long hair was the man she had fallen in love with. The man who had broken her heart. Then his friend Rosalie had warned her that Raoul was not all he seemed, but she'd been so deep in love she'd ignored it. Or at least hadn't listened to it properly. So she'd been stunned to find that her own teasing nickname for him was the very one that was used in the international business world to describe his ruthless, cold-blooded determination to make a profit.

The Corsican Bandit was the man she was dealing with now. Because of that, she was going to have to tread carefully. And her sister's arrival had reminded her that there was more than her own future at stake.

'Enjoy your day!' she said over-brightly, praying it didn't sound as fake to him as it did to her own ears. 'Come on, Ciara, we have lots to do!'

Moving to the open doorway, Raoul stood, eyes narrowed, feet firmly planted wide apart, as he watched the two women walk away across the lush green field towards Blacklands House. He wouldn't have known the two women were sisters if he hadn't been told, he reflected. Ciara was shorter, with more rounded curves, and her hair was a glorious red-gold. Just Pierre's type, damn him.

'She's so young, Raoul, and so lovely.' Marina's words echoed in his head. 'And twenty years younger than me—it's no wonder he's entranced. I wish I'd never given her the job as nanny!'

Deep in his pockets, his hands clenched into tight, aggressive fists. The image of Imogen and her sister walking so close together, arms linked without a care in the world, it seemed, brought back a bitter remembrance of that photograph in the papers.

The Scandalous O'Sullivan Sisters. His breath hissed in between clenched teeth.

Yesterday had been just the start. A preliminary survey to get the lie of the land. Tomorrow he would put his plan into operation and he would set himself to bring down the O'Sullivan family, one by one.

Starting with Imogen.

CHAPTER THREE

IT WAS FAR worse than she had thought. Imogen had tried to imagine all sorts of things that Raoul might have against her sister, but never this. Her blood ran cold. It was bad enough to think that Raoul Cardini had appeared out of her past, to be the spectre at her wedding feast, but to realise that her younger sister too was caught up in the dark shadows he had brought with him made her nerves knot in her stomach.

'Why didn't you tell me before now?'

'I couldn't,' Ciara admitted, and Imogen was shocked to see how white she looked. 'I didn't really know you when all this happened.'

That was her mother's fault, Imogen reflected, feeling the raw scrape of bitterness on her soul. Lizzie O'Sullivan had abandoned her marriage when she'd run off with her much younger, much more glamorous lover. Arturo had never wanted children, but Lizzie had persuaded him to take her toddler daughter with them. She had always struggled to get close to Imogen whose bookish, studious nature was nothing like her mother's. Besides, the elder girl had inherited her father's love for horses and the stud that provided their livelihood, while her mother loathed and feared the great, enormous beasts. Determined to break off all ties with the family she had left behind in Ireland, Lizzie had never even told Ciara that she had a sister—and to hide it she had adopted Arturo's name for the family.

The memory of the long years not knowing anything about her little sister still had the power to hurt Imogen. When Lizzie had finally resurfaced, abandoned by her lover and left without the financial support she had looked to him for, it was to demand her right to one half of the O'Sullivan 'fortune'. A fortune that had dwindled dangerously while their father Joe had taken his hands off the reins and let the stud run down desperately. Her mother's demands had threatened to bring bankruptcy crashing down on their heads, but Joe had been determined to pay her off to get her out of his life, even though it had taken every last penny and put the stud even further into debt. That was why Imogen had finally agreed to Adnan's businesslike suggestion of a marriage of convenience between them.

The one good thing that had come out of her mother's reappearance was that it had brought the sisters back in touch with each other. Only then had Imogen discovered that Ciara and her mother had been estranged for some time and that her sister had been working as a nanny in Australia, but the job had come to an end and she was now living in London.

At last, Imogen had finally made contact with her again and they had arranged to meet up. It had only been in the time she'd spent away from Blacklands and the stresses of her father's gambling addiction that she'd noticed her period was late. A pregnancy test had confirmed her fears.

Imogen nodded sadly. 'We might be sisters, but we were complete strangers at the start.'

'And we didn't have enough time to get to know each other when I was heading for that new job in Melbourne.'

A brief visit to the stud before she'd left was all they'd managed to fit in. That was why she'd had such high hopes when Ciara had come to the wedding. Perhaps now they could build real bridges and finally erase the separation of the past.

'Then you were so ill…'

This time Imogen had to bite down hard on her lower lip to hold back the pain that almost escaped her.

'I don't think I'd have got through losing my baby without you.'

Ciara had held her tight when Imogen had endured the agony of an ectopic pregnancy, losing the baby she had conceived during those magical two weeks on the island of Corsica. It had meant so much to have another female to hold her and murmur soothing words. She had endured so many long years without a mother's comfort, so a sister's love had been a wonderful solace when she most needed it. She had never been able to share anything of her sadness with her father. He had been busy driving himself down the path to destruction, turning to the bottle for solace, and had never even picked up on her unhappiness.

She only wished she could have brought her sister home to see the stud as it had been, if not in its glory days, at least in some degree of stability and success. But Ciara had only been in London temporarily. She'd been looking forward to creating a new life in Australia.

Ciara had never shared just what was troubling her when she had returned home. Did that mean Imogen hadn't really been there when her sister had needed her? Had her own misery blinded her to the way Ciara was feeling when she had lost her job—and the circumstances in which she'd lost it?

Imogen had never suspected that Raoul Cardini was the brother-in-law of Pierre Moreau, the man who had caused her sister so many problems, dragged her name through the mud and ultimately sacked her in disgrace. Now that she did know, it seemed obvious that Raoul would delight in making Ciara pay for what he saw as the insult to his family, his sister and her children. The tension that had been dragging at her insides just knowing Raoul was here, bringing with him those dark shadows of the past they had once shared, twisted into tight, painful knots. What did Raoul plan to tell Adnan? Because he did mean to expose someone and something, that much was certain.

Imogen was determined to make sure Raoul did nothing to hurt Ciara. It was the way she could make up for not realising just how low her sister had been at that first meeting.

She'd been trying to find Raoul ever since she'd made her way back to the stud but there hadn't been a trace of the damn man. In the end, she'd had to take the chance that he still had the same number as the one she'd been weak enough to keep on her own phone in a last attempt to reach him.

What would Adnan do if Raoul revealed all he knew about her own past, and her sister's? Would he go through with the wedding? Or would he decide that even their friendship, and the prospect of keeping his promise to his grandfather to provide him with an heir, cost too much at the price of tying himself to her scandalous family? He was a friend, but was he that much of a friend?

Raoul's phone beeped again, for perhaps the tenth time that afternoon, and a twitch of a smile curled the corners of his mouth as he saw Imogen's name as the sender of the incoming text.

We need to talk.

'Answer it,' the man with him said easily.

Raoul shook his head, his shoulders lifting in a shrug of indifference.

'It's not important—it can wait.'

'No, answer it. I'll make us another drink.'

As his companion got out of his seat and strolled out of the room, Raoul reached lazily for the phone that was still buzzing annoyingly.

We have things we need to talk about.

His thumb flew over the keyboard, casually creating his reply.

I'm busy.

He waited a nicely calculated moment, then added:

I'm talking to Al Makthabi right now.

After that he deliberately switched off the phone and dropped it into his jacket pocket.

Just how long could Raoul be talking to Adnan—and about what? Imogen stared out of her bedroom window and down onto the winding drive that led to the main house, her fingers drumming against the window pane.

Her phone calls had gone straight to voicemail, her texts unanswered after that final declaration that he was with her fiancé, and she had heard nothing, seen nothing of him, for the rest of the day.

With a sigh, she rested her aching head on the hand that rested on the window pane—a hand that had been carefully manicured, the nails painted a delicate pink, ready for the moment when Adnan would place a gold ring on it and make her his wife. Behind her, the beautiful white silk dress hung outside the wardrobe, protected by a cotton covering. Imogen hadn't been able to bring herself even to look at it since the dressmaker had delivered it. She had always had contradictory feelings about it, knowing it was part of a wedding of convenience, not a true, romantic marriage of love. But now she felt the nerves tightening in her throat and stomach as her eyes blurred after too long spent watching to see when Raoul would appear.

'I think I need an early night, to be fresh for tomorrow,' she'd told her father, knowing there was no chance at all she would sleep.

Even if Raoul returned soon, Ciara was still out somewhere in the dark, wet night, the sudden storm and driving rain taking all trace of summer from the atmosphere. She would never be able to settle until she knew her sister was safe.

The glare of headlights drew her attention, warning her that a car was arriving. Squinting through the rain, she saw the sleek, dark vehicle draw to a halt at the door and three male figures get out, heads bent as they dashed through the rain and up the steps.

'At last!'

Now, surely, she would have a chance to try to get the truth out of Raoul, to find out just what fiendish scheme was in his mind. Would he let the wedding go ahead tomorrow or did he plan to spoil it somehow?

The shudder that ran through her was as if the window had suddenly blown wide open, letting the rain in. She had changed into her nightwear when she'd come up to the room, but now the strappy nightie felt too cold, too little protection against the chill of the night, so she turned from the window, reaching for her robe as an extra layer of warmth. Adnan had been one of the men who'd arrived; she recognised the distinctive leather jacket he wore. Her father had been another. How could she manage this without being seen by these two men? She couldn't bear to wait until everyone was asleep. The burn of apprehension and fear was bad enough already.

Her question was answered by her father's voice down in the hall declaring that he had a fine whisky to share.

'We could have a nightcap...?' he offered jovially.

'Not for me, thanks. I'm going to turn in.' That was Raoul; the sexy accent made it clear.

As heavy male footsteps came up the stairs, the sound of the library door swinging shut behind the other two men made Imogen sag against the wall in relief. At last she was free to make her way to Raoul's room, and she wasn't going to leave without some much-needed answers.

But she couldn't head for Raoul's bedroom openly—across the main landing, straight to his door. That would be just asking for trouble.

Luckily, Blacklands House was old enough to have many secrets, amongst which were the hidden passages that linked one room to another by a series of stone steps. Much of her childhood had been spent running along these passages, learning how to get into them from every room and where each one came out.

The fake wall beside the bookcase was easy to open if you pressed one of the plaster roses that decorated it. Slipping inside, she made her way along the passage in darkness, bare feet making no sound. It was as she pushed slightly open the secret entry door into Raoul's room that she heard the main door open again down in the hall. At last, Ciara was home. Now she needed to make sure that her sister's fears—and her own—could be put behind them. Somehow, she had to convince Raoul not to ruin the wedding, or to drag Ciara's name any further through the mud than it had been already.

The roar of the elderly shower from the bathroom hid the sound of the door sliding closed behind her as she crept into the room.

Raoul reached up and switched off the shower with a violent snap of his wrist. It had taken an age for the damn thing to run even close to warm, never mind hot, and he was far from feeling the relaxation he had hoped for.

Grabbing a towel, he rubbed it roughly over his soaking hair, thankful that the short, cropped cut retained little of the water. It was so damn cold in this ramshackle place; no hint of warmth in the old-fashioned bathroom.

'Nom de Dieu!' he swore explosively, tossing

the damp towel aside and reaching for another, slinging it around his hips and fastening it tight. It was supposed to be summer!

But it wasn't just the weather that was turning his mood sour, he knew. It was being here at all that was the problem. Being here, surrounded by the beauty of the countryside, the magnificence of the spectacular animals that grazed in the field, and knowing that the whole enterprise was rotten to the core; that there was no money to support the business and everything was in hock to the bank. Even the magnificent stallion Blackjack… Knowing that he had been conned into paying stud fees for a horse that didn't actually belong to Joe O'Sullivan burned like acid in his gut.

Rubbing the back of his hand across his face to wipe away the moisture, he padded across the tiled floor, wrenching the handle to yank the door open. The financial situation couldn't be any worse, so Imogen had clearly turned to the oldest trick in the book—marrying the nearest really wealthy man in order to help clear her family's debts. The same trick that she'd tried to pull on him when she'd discovered that he was not the simple olive farmer he'd claimed to be. Obviously, the financial problems had already begun to bite back then.

'Damn her to hell!'

He had known this—most of this—before he'd arrived. It was the reason he was here, after all. But it had all seemed so much simpler before he'd left Corsica. The woman who had tried to get her hands on his fortune had now found someone else equally wealthy to marry. Someone else whose child, it seemed, she was prepared to have when the truth was that she had already got rid of her first baby—his child. Tossed it aside because its wealthy father wasn't going to fall into the trap she'd laid for him.

But now, she'd found someone who would do just as she wanted. Someone who would marry her, pour money into this downtrodden estate and pay off the bills.

He had come here to stop that wedding.

But things had got so much more complicated since he'd arrived. He'd seen Imogen and her sister. He'd met the man Imogen was going to marry, and—damn it to hell—he liked Adnan Al Makthabi. Respected him. Adnan was the type of man he'd like as a friend—if he had such a thing.

'Raoul…'

A voice, soft, uncertain and shockingly familiar, broke into his thoughts, bringing his head up. Dashing any last trace of water from his eyes, he swung round sharply to face her.

It was as if his heated sexual memories of their time together, the ones that had made the inadequate temperature of the shower a positive bonus, had brought her out of the past, conjured her up as a real person here in his room.

But how the devil had she got in here? He was between her and the exit and he knew he'd turned the key in the bedroom door when he'd gone into the bathroom. Yet there she was, tall and slender in a deep crimson robe wrapped tightly around her, tied at the waist. She was standing against the wall, half-hidden by the heavy, embroidered drape of the curtains around one of the carved posters of the bed.

'What the hell are you doing here?'

He saw the way her breasts rose and fell under

the delicate silk of her robe with every sharp, uneven breath she took. The wide, wide eyes were clear and sapphire blue even in the dusky shadows, and her mouth was partly open, as if to speak—*or to kiss*, his rebellious thoughts whispered to him. She'd always been beautiful. Hell, she was still beautiful—more so than before, if that were possible.

She had once worn a scarlet dress that had been little more than the nightgown she had on under the robe, but it had been short and sweet with a flippy sort of hem that had shown off her long legs. He had revelled in watching the pale, Celtic skin slowly tan to a subtle, sexy golden brown after days in the sun. The kick of lust at his groin was unwelcome and ill-timed—and appallingly distracting. The white towel suddenly felt like no covering at all and he shifted uncomfortably, pulling it tighter at the waist, tucking the edge in again.

'I said, what the hell are you doing here?' he demanded, his voice rougher than before as he fought with the temptation his memories were throwing at him.

He saw her flinch, blink hard, but then she drew herself up to face him defiantly, blue eyes clashing with his.

'I came to talk to you.'

'About what, exactly?'

She had spent all yesterday trying to ignore him. Today had been the reverse of that, bombarding him with text messages and demands that they meet. It was obvious she was on edge, even if she was trying to look down her pretty little nose at him.

'About…?'

The rap at the door was loud and staccato, and it came in the same moment as her response, so that he could barely hear the word. Imogen broke off abruptly, eyes going to the big wooden door behind her, a faint questioning frown creasing the space between her brows.

'Monsieur Cardini? Are you in there?

'Ciara!'

Her sister's name was a sound of pure shock and Imogen looked around frantically, clearly hunting for somewhere to hide.

'I need to talk to you.'

'Another one,' Raoul drawled, one black eyebrow drifting upwards cynically. 'My, but I am popular tonight.'

'Not *popular*!' Imogen's outburst was a hiss of fury, like that of an angry cat.

'Open the door—please. Let me in. I need to talk to you.'

'She mustn't know I'm here!'

'Monsieur Cardini…' Ciara begged. 'We can't let things go on like this.'

'Un moment...'

He was about to suggest to Imogen that she hide, but she had taken action herself, stepping further back, closer to the wall, pressing herself flat up against it. She reached out and caught hold of the embroidered drapes, tugging at them and pulling them closer around her until she was totally concealed.

'Please…' Her sister was clearly getting anxious on the other side of the door.

'All right.' Not sparing another glance at the spot where Imogen stood hidden, he turned the key in the lock and pulled open the door.

Ciara must have been right up against the wood

because, as he opened it, she almost tumbled into the room. Her red-gold hair was wet from the rain and was flattened against her skull, and her face still had traces of damp along her brow and cheekbones, the waft of cool evening air coming into the room with her.

'What the devil is this?'

He'd had enough of intruders in his room, enough of the O'Sullivan sisters invading his life, rocking the balance of his thoughts.

'I need to talk to you—to try and sort things out so that you don't spoil my sister's wedding, and— Oh!'

The small cry of shock was because she had only just registered his half-naked state, the towel hitched around his hips. The rush of pink into her cheeks was unlike the response of her sister, who had merely regarded him with the sort of cool control that had set his teeth on edge. But the knowledge that that sister was behind him, hidden behind the heavy curtains, only aggravated his already irritated mood. He brought his hand down in a slashing sort of movement, wanting to cut short the hesitation and get to the point.

'Mademoiselle O'Sullivan—say what you have to say and then leave me in peace.'

Did she hear the noise behind her, the footsteps on the stairs? If she didn't, he certainly did, and the sounds destroyed any last grip on his patience.

'Speak!'

Behind the concealing curtain, Imogen winced instinctively as she heard that cold bite of anger in Raoul's voice. She'd heard that once before, when she had tried to persuade him to continue their relationship beyond the weeks he had prescribed. It meant trouble—ice-cold, ruthless trouble.

Silently she willed Ciara to say her piece and *go*.

'I'm here to beg you not to do anything. Not to say anything.'

The quaver in her sister's voice told Imogen that Ciara had recognised the danger in Raoul's tone, even if she didn't know the full story behind it. But she had never seen the tall, dark Corsican's eyes blaze with golden fire, the way his nostrils flared, his mouth clamping tight over the anger burning inside, turning it into savage ice with the force of his control.

Imogen prayed her sister would never have to experience the way it felt to be on the receiving end of that sizzling glare and feel it burn her almost to ashes.

'About what?'

'About me… Don't tell anyone about my—my past. Because I need you not to spoil things for Imogen and Adnan. Don't ruin her marriage… please.'

'And you think that what her silly little sister got up to would ruin Imogen's chance of marriage? Why would that be?'

Imogen shivered to hear the coldness in Raoul's voice. Ciara was too young, too sweet, too innocent to contend with a sophisticated monster like Raoul Cardini. Wasn't that why she had got herself entangled with that hateful womaniser Pierre Moreau? She had emerged from that encounter bruised and battered, and only now was just beginning to put her life back together again.

'I couldn't bear it if you said anything. Imogen's been through enough already. My father doesn't know, nor does Adnan, and…'

'But Imogen does?'

Now Imogen could see where his cold, dark, vengeful thoughts were going. He had always seen her as nothing but a gold-digger, worth no more than a brief holiday fling and some hot summer sex before tossing her aside. He'd been happy to walk away without a single backward glance, but then he'd obviously discovered that her family wasn't out of his life after all, that her sister was the nanny who had been accused of almost breaking up his sister's marriage—the source of the *Nookie with the Nanny* headlines that had called open season on Pierre Moreau and his wife Marina.

And the proud Corsican was not going to stand for that.

'Monsieur Cardini—please—I'll do anything if you'll just let Imogen and Adnan…'

But that was more than Imogen could take. She couldn't stay here in hiding and listen to the break in her sister's voice, the savage ice in Raoul's. She couldn't let Ciara fight for her sister's future, for what she thought was Imogen's happiness, by taking the blame on her own slender shoulders.

Particularly not when the marriage Ciara was fighting to save was not the love match she obviously believed it to be. Now she regretted letting her sister believe in the delusion that this was a true romance.

'Ciara—no!'

Imogen was rushing forward as she spoke, pushing her way out from behind the heavy curtains, struggling to get free.

She stumbled out into the room, blinking at the light after being hidden in the darkness. In the haste of her movements, her robe came adrift and was tugged backwards, pulling the sides apart, the belt open. Her hair had been dragged loose as well, tumbling round her shoulders, falling across her face, but she couldn't care.

'No—don't say any more. I'm dealing with everything. Raoul and I…'

Her voice trailed off, dropping into silence as she blundered into the hard, solid form of Raoul Cardini standing right in the middle of the room.

'Imogen!' he exclaimed, his voice a bark of reproof.

'Are you sure about that whisky, Cardini…?'

To her horror, that question came from her father, overly cheerful and still some way down the corridor, looking for someone to share his nightcap.

'Oh, Immi!' Ciara's voice clashed with his but hers was a sound of shock and consternation.

Even as she caught her sister's stunned exclamation, Imogen heard her father's voice again, closer now. Desperately she struggled to brush back her tangled hair, sweep it out of her eyes and focus on the scene that was before her.

'Imogen?'

That was her father who was inside the door now, one hand on Ciara's arm, the other reaching up to cover his mouth as if to hold back further expressions of total disbelief.

It was bad enough being caught by her father and sister like this, on the night before her wedding in another man's bedroom, in her nightclothes with her hair in disarray… But as her thoughts reeled, and she wondered how to explain the situation without making it any worse, her eyes cleared and she saw that it already was far worse. The worst.

It was not just her father who had come into the room. Someone else had been drawn by Ciara's voice. Someone else was out in the corridor, his tall frame blending into the shadows, his battered leather jacket giving him away at once.

'*Imogen!* What the hell is going on?' thundered a voice that could only belong to a savagely shocked and furious Adnan Al Makthabi.

CHAPTER FOUR

'F-FATHER...'

It was all Imogen could manage, even that one word being almost beyond her. What was impossible was actually looking into the corridor, after that one brief, horrified glance that had met with the blazing glare of the man who was supposed to be her bridegroom tomorrow.

Or was that today? The clock out in the hallway at the bottom of the stairs was already beginning to strike midnight, the deep, booming notes reverberating up the stairwell towards them.

'Don't you know it's bad luck for the groom to see his bride before the actual wedding...?' Raoul drawled cynically.

Which wasn't very far from the mark. Her brain was whirling in a lethal combination of shock and disbelief, thought processes shattered. Her eyes wouldn't focus either so she couldn't actually see

Adnan's face, only her sister's white, stunned expression and her father's features drawn in appalled disbelief.

'What wedding?' Adnan tossed at her, hard enough to cut through the air in the room and making it difficult to breathe.

'Our—' She swallowed audibly. 'Obviously *our* wedding…'

'Nothing obvious about that from where I'm standing.'

'But Adnan…'

Everyone else had frozen into silent figures in the room. But then just as she tried to move forward, past Raoul, she found that she was grabbed, her arm gripped in a punishing hold that pulled her back against a warm, powerful, masculine form.

It was the feel of the heat of his skin against her now exposed back, the thud of his heart underneath the hard frame of his ribcage that shocked her into silence. She had forgotten—how could she have forgotten?—that, while she was wearing only the half-on, half-off nightdress with her robe falling down her back, Raoul was *half-*

naked, barely covered by the white towel knotted at his narrow waist. Pressed up against him like this, the scent of his clean skin overlaid with the tang of lemon from his shampoo curled around her from behind, enclosing her in a sensual haze, scrambling her thoughts even further.

'Adnan…' she tried again, but the burning image of what he must be seeing dried her throat so that no further words would come out.

She was grateful for the blurring of her vision so she couldn't see the anger, the betrayal, in his face. The wedding might not have been any sort of love match, but Adnan was her friend. He had also offered to help her out of the hard place in which her father had dropped her and the rest of her family. He deserved better than this.

'This isn't what it seems,' she managed miserably, then, forcing a new strength into her voice, 'Tell them, Raoul.'

Tell them, Raoul. The man who held her registered that. It had come out like a command. She might as well have accompanied it with a snap of her fingers. Obviously, she expected him to obey.

Equally obviously, that was the last thing he planned right now.

For one thing, he had never jumped to any woman's command and he didn't intend to start now. For another, one which was starting to become much more important, the feel of her pressed up against him like this was scrambling his thoughts. He had forgotten how it felt to be this close to her. To feel the soft, warm silk of her skin against his. The black fall of her hair slithered over his shoulders, his chest, delicate strands of it catching against the evening's growth of beard and tangling in the stubble. And her neat behind was pressed close up against him, his erection against the cleft between her buttocks.

The effect on him would be obvious if she moved. And that would clearly only make things so much worse. Not that he gave a damn if it ruined Imogen's chances. Wasn't that what he had come here for in the first place?

'No need for it to be explained,' he drawled, pulling Imogen back against him as she tried to move away towards her fiancé.

If Al Makthabi was still her fiancé after this.

Surely the other man would thank him for freeing him from marriage to a woman who was only after him for his money?

'This is exactly what it seems.'

He spoke over Imogen's gasp of outraged indignation, tightening his grip warningly on the arms she tried to pull away from him. He caught her tiny murmur of discomfort and immediately loosened his grip just a touch. Not enough to let her break away, but enough not to bruise that soft white skin that was making it hellishly difficult to concentrate on what he was saying.

What he really wanted was to tell them all to get to hell out of here, to press his mouth against the fine line of her exposed neck, kiss it, let his tongue slip out to taste it, press nibbling little bites…

Hell, no!

Brutally, he dragged his mind back from the wanton path it seemed determined to follow, the shockingly sensual little wriggle that Imogen gave against him revealing without words that she was aware of the effect she was having on him. The battle he was fighting to control his most basic feelings roughened his voice so it sounded harsher than he had intended.

'Imogen came to see me—we knew each other before, didn't we, *chérie*?'

'No!'

Imogen couldn't believe what was happening, what he was saying. How could he possibly be calling her *darling* when it was so far from any sort of truth? Particularly when it was hissed in her ear like the voice of the serpent in the Garden of Eden.

'Oui, ma chère.'

Long fingers stroked down her arm, making her writhe in uncontrolled response. A tiny, abandoned moan escaped her, sliding out before she could bite down hard on her lower lip to hold it back. How could this be happening?

But she couldn't suppress the red alert flaring in all her senses; couldn't bring that yearning memory under control. Behind her, Raoul's strength supported her, his heat surrounded her, his mouth drifted across her neck at the point where her pulse throbbed in desperate, uncontrolled response. Even now, with no trace of privacy in the room. With her father, her sister… Oh, dear heaven—*Adnan!*

To her horror, she found herself closing her eyes in response then frantically forcing them open. And wishing she'd never done that when she caught the raw savage rage in Adnan's eyes, the snarl of fury that twisted his mouth.

'You were lovers.'

It was thrown straight into her face and there was no way she could avoid it. It was as if the ground had opened up beneath her, throwing her down, deep down into hell, and she couldn't possibly escape. She couldn't deny it either. To do so would be to lie to Adnan and she couldn't do that. She owed him the truth if nothing else.

Rough and raw, she dragged in a painful breath to give her the strength to speak. At the same time, unexpectedly, she felt the change in Raoul's grip, the new way he was holding her. Still tight, but somehow stronger, supporting rather than restraining her.

'Yes…' she sighed, sad and low. 'Yes, we were.'

Raoul hadn't expected that. She sensed it from a new tension in the long body against which hers was pressed. He clearly hadn't expected her to speak the truth. But what else could she do? She had valued Adnan's friendship for so long. She couldn't wrong him now.

The words fell into icy silence. The only sound in the room was her own heart thudding heavily in her ears, the blood pulsing along her veins. There was the tiniest sensation of Raoul's breath, warm and soft on her neck, and shockingly it felt like a touch of comfort in a world where everything had turned black.

'But…' She tried to start again but her voice had no strength and no one could hear her whisper because of the snarl of icy fury from Adnan that covered it.

'You're welcome to her.'

The words were tossed into the room, cold, stark, totally indifferent. And they were directed at Raoul, flying past her as if she no longer existed.

She didn't exist any more—not for Adnan. She had no doubt about that. If she needed any further proof, it was there in the way he turned on his heel and strode away, angry footsteps echoing down the corridor.

She tried to tug herself away from Raoul's hold.

'Let me go!' she cried, turning her head to direct it at his cheek.

But that was a terrible mistake. It brought her face so close to his that the scent of his skin warmed her senses; and, when she cried out her rage, her lips actually grazed the stubble covering the rich, olive skin of his jaw. She could taste him against her tongue and the rush of memory almost took her legs from under her. She would have sagged against him if it weren't for the sudden tightening of his grip, the strength of his muscles supporting her.

'Let me go!'

'Not if you're going after him.'

'Going after him? Don't be stupid! Did you hear what he said? Do you think he'd want me now?'

She twisted round in Raoul's arms, needing to face him, then immediately wished she hadn't. The movement brought her hard up against him, her pelvis crushed against his so she couldn't be unaware of the swollen evidence of his arousal beneath the inadequate concealment of the towel. The heat of it, the burning sensation, froze her in total shock.

'Let me… I'll go after him…'

It was Ciara who spoke, turning and running out the door, following where Adnan had marched away just moments before. Imogen heard her dashing along the corridor, down the stairs, and then her steps faded into silence.

'No point,' she tried to respond, but no one was listening. Outside, there was the roar of the powerful engine of Adnan's car and the spurt of gravel under the wheels as he sped away.

'Immi…'

She had forgotten her father was there.

Joe O'Sullivan's stunned expression was just too much for her battered and bruised mind to take in. Her senses were assailed by the strength of Raoul's arms around her, the rise and fall of his powerful ribcage as he breathed, the dark glint of watchful golden eyes. If she inhaled, she took in his scent; if she moved her head, she felt the scrape of his bristled chin. And all the time there was that hot, hard, demanding pressure into the cradle of her hips, reminding her of wilder times, dangerous days when she had lost herself in the strength and fire of this man's passion.

'Oh, Immi…'

The sound of her name from her father again barely reached her through the whirling confusion in her thoughts. It also had a fraying edge on the word, one sadly she knew all too well. Joe O'Sullivan had been celebrating his daughter's upcoming wedding—and his own prospective freedom from fear and debt—just a little too well. As she blinked away the sense of apprehension in her own eyes, she saw Raoul look down at her, dark and intent, his focus fixed on her and nowhere else.

'Get out,' he said, cold and stark.

For a moment, Imogen thought his words were addressed to her and she lifted her head to try to look around. Then immediately wished she hadn't. The movement brought her eyes round to the mirrored door in the huge, old-fashioned wardrobe that stood against the far wall, with her image reflected in it. And the sight of that reflection brought the heat rushing up her body, scorching through every cell.

Was that what Adnan had seen? If it was then it was no wonder he had walked out without a single glance back, their arrangement, their friendship shattered in a moment. He must have seen that wanton-looking woman in another man's arms, her hair tossed and tangled down her back, the make-up she had forgotten to take off in her haste to talk with Raoul smudged under her eyes. The robe had been dragged apart and hung halfway off one shoulder, the thin strap of her nightgown following it to drape partway down her arm.

No wonder Adnan had stalked away. No wonder he had turned his back on her—and the future they had hoped to secure for Blacklands. Guilt tore at her conscience and blended fiercely with fury at the way Raoul had behaved, the way he'd trapped her here like this with her father.

'Dad...please,' she begged, unable to turn and look at him, unable once again to drag her gaze away from Raoul's burning eyes. The hypnotic hold he had on her was far stronger than the muscular grip that held her so close. 'Go now.'

'But Immi—what about the wedding? What—?'

'Go.' It was Raoul's voice, flat and emphatic, no room for argument. 'Go now.'

'Dad—please do as he says.'

If she could hear the pleading note in her father's voice, then surely Raoul could too. Or was that just because she knew what was behind it? How much had depended on her wedding, and how much would be ruined now that Adnan would never go through with the event.

'Go!' Raoul repeated, his tone darkening dangerously.

Imogen didn't have to look back over her shoulder to see her father's expression. She could sense it in the quality of his silence. The bristling defiance was combined with an underlying fear and the need to protect himself from the consequences of his own irresponsible actions. It had been there in his face, in his tone, when she had told him that she was going to marry Adnan. He'd known he shouldn't be asking this of her, but he hadn't been able to hold back the relief at the thought that there was a chance of being rescued from the desperate situation he had found himself in. It was no wonder he was in this mess; he was fine with the horses he knew and loved—but financial problems and the real world were way beyond him. He had never been a strong man emotionally, which was why she had never told him about her pregnancy and its tragic end.

'If you're sure, Immi. Well, you might put some clothes on, young man!'

With this last attempt at defiant challenge, Joe turned on his heel and left, the speed of his departure betraying how glad he was to be on his way.

It was that final retort that proved to be too much for Imogen. Suddenly, the appalling sense of tension that had been twisting in her stomach since the moment of Ciara's arrival snapped, shattering her composure and taking her sense of control with it.

'Put some clothes on!' she gasped, fighting the wave of near-hysterical laughter that overtook her. Her eyes closed, her head bent as she struggled with the giggles that swept through her. 'Y-young man!'

'It is some time since I was called that.'

Raoul's tone was wry. The tiny touch of humour, totally unexpected in his voice, was too much, too full of memories to cope with, breaking her in a very different way. Imogen stiffened and pulled back against his hold and away from the warmth and strength of his body. It was only when she put that space between them that she recognised how, weakly and dangerously, she had given in to the sense of comfort that being held had brought. A lying, deceptive sense of comfort, because Raoul's arms offered no safety. Instead, he was the real source of menace, the true threat to her peace of mind.

How could she have been weak enough to let herself even think of surrendering to that malign temptation? The shock must have rattled her brain more than she'd imagined.

'Dad was right—you should put some clothes on,' she said sharply. 'If you think I'm going to talk to you with you looking like that…'

'Why?' It was wickedly cool and smooth, curling round her like perfumed smoke. 'Am I distracting you?'

Totally. The sight of so much beautiful skin, the haze of black hair that shadowed the muscular chest tracing a path down towards the point where it disappeared under the immaculate white towelling that was fastened around his narrow waist, was too much of a reminder of the way it had felt to have his hard body, the heated thrust of his manhood, pressed against her. It sent the blood rushing through her body and thundering inside her head.

'Not at all,' she managed with a pretence of carelessness. 'But I think we've caused enough scandal for tonight. And if we're going to talk…'

'Are we?' Raoul pushed a lean hand through the crisp, damp strands of his hair as he raised one dark brow interrogatively. 'What do we need to talk about?'

'Well…'

She'd spoken without thinking. Stupidly, it seemed. Raoul had managed to turn her whole life upside down and inside out. He'd sent her fiancé away in a black rage, breaking their engagement. He'd ruined the prospect of the wedding that was supposed to be happening tomorrow—*today*, she realised as she remembered she'd heard the chime of midnight. The wedding that was supposed to have saved them all. It was only now she recognised that somewhere, naively, deep down inside, she'd allowed herself to think that perhaps he might do something to help.

What could have put such a crazy idea into her head? And yet where could she go now that her future lay in ruins at her feet? The idea of going back to her room, to the emptiness and darkness, to face the loneliness and destruction of what she'd done, was more than she could bear.

'I'm sorry. There's nothing, of course. I'll leave you.'

'Non!'

Somehow the command sounded much more emphatic in his native language. Imogen flinched inside as it reminded her of the time they had once spent together, the way she had tried to learn French to be able to talk to him and to understand the signs and the notices on the sun-warmed island where they'd met. She'd also hoped it would help her understand him. Fat chance of that!

'N-non?'

'Perhaps we do need to talk.'

He needed to get out of this towel and into some more concealing clothing. The effect she was still having on his body was so primal that if she came close again she would feel the evidence of how aroused she made him just by breathing. Hell, no, that was a mistake. Thinking of her breathing inevitably brought his gaze to the top of that flame-coloured nightgown, still exposed by the way the silken robe hung half off her shoulders. The smooth curves of pale skin and the deep cleft of her cleavage were tormenting temptation in themselves, and the way those curves rose and fell with the uneven, heightened pace of her breathing threatened to destroy his ability to think at all.

'And I will put some clothes on.'

Now, what was that look? Relief? Or annoyance? He wasn't arrogant enough to call it disappointment, no matter how tempting it had been to tease her over that a short time before.

'You too.'

As he moved past her he paused to lift the edges of the robe up and over her shoulders, tugging them together to remove the temptation of her breasts. The ragged way she was breathing brought those soft curves up to meet his hands, brushing against his fingers for a moment so that he had to complete the movement with an awkward jerk, letting the silk drop into place as he stepped back and away abruptly.

'Help yourself to a drink.'

He waved a hand in the direction of the rich red wine he'd left to breathe on the dressing table as, impatient to get out of the way of temptation, he snatched up the jeans and shirt that he'd left on the bed on his way into the bathroom.

There wasn't time to shower all over again, no matter how much he needed the pounding of icy water to suppress the hungry demand that was making his body ache with discomfort. For one thing, Imogen knew he'd just come out of the shower when she'd stumbled into the room.

His pulse rate skyrocketed at the memory of the way she had looked then, appearing like a fantasy in his dream just when he'd been imagining her, remembering that last night in Corsica, before she had turned into another woman, one so like the greedy gold-diggers he'd come up against too often already.

She'd even used the same words that Alice had spoken: 'I need to tell you something. I can't let you go…'

No, damn it, no! He forced his eyes away from the shower and instead contented himself with filling the sink with cold water and dunking his head and face deep into it. It did little to quell the throbbing pulse in his groin, but it did force him to clear his mind and try to think as coldly and rationally about things as he could. The memory of the way Alice had used him, taken his love and cast it aside, did the rest.

This was not how he had expected the evening to go. Though, if he were honest with himself, he hadn't really *expected* anything.

Certainly not the sudden appearance of Imogen in his room, bringing with her too many memories, too many hopes he had once cherished.

Hopes he had once been young enough and fool enough to believe in.

The thought of those naïve dreams threatened to distract him from the path he had determined on. The path that had unexpectedly opened up so clearly and easily in the space of the last hour. When he had planned his revenge on Imogen O'Sullivan he had never really anticipated it being handed to him on a plate like this. But he intended to take full advantage of it.

CHAPTER FIVE

'HELP YOURSELF TO a drink.'

Imogen gritted her teeth against the irritation those words caused her. The casual invitation drifted over his shoulder as he walked away from her into the *en suite*. As if he was the host here and she a mere visitor.

Which she might well be soon, cold reality reminded her. The marriage of convenience to Adnan had been their last chance to save the stud, her father's reputation and her own future. Now those plans lay in ashes, the hope she'd had disappearing out of the door with Adnan in that black rage.

Who could blame him? When she thought of the scene that must have met her fiancé's eyes—her *former* fiancé's eyes—just minutes before, her skin burned, her eyes stinging with hot tears of shame. She had lost Adnan's friendship as well as everything else, she knew. His powerful male pride would never stand for seeing her in another man's bedroom, in his arms—and both of them half-dressed.

Shaking fingers moved over the rumpled silk of her robe, feeling how, even now, her insubstantial clothing was still not fully restored to any degree of order. The memory of the cold, indifferent way that Raoul had hauled her robe around her—the speed with which he had pulled his hands away as if, once their audience had gone, it disgusted him to touch her—made her feel as if something cold and slimy had slithered over her skin. Once, he hadn't been able to wait long enough to peel her clothes from her body, but had ripped them away in the heat of hunger. Several of her dresses had ended up as mere shreds of cotton, discarded on the floor.

This time, he had shown the same need to have her cover herself, had done the job for her with a rough coldness that brutally contradicted the desire she'd thought she'd felt when he was pressed up against her back. Obviously, that had been the primitive, basic response of a red-blooded man to any half-tolerable female. But then, when he had realised precisely which woman he had been dealing with, his whole mood had changed in the space of a heartbeat.

With an abrupt movement, Imogen yanked her robe up around her, belting it as tightly as she could, then made her way across to the table where the bottle of wine stood next to two glasses.

Two? Who had he been expecting? The question froze her hand, leaving it suspended in mid-air as she forced herself to consider the question. Had Raoul had an assignation here? But he didn't know anyone in Ireland. Or did he?

He'd said that he'd visited Ireland once before. Was it possible he had met some other woman? In a bar, maybe, as he had once met her, inviting her back to the house, to his room…

Having previously not dared to risk the effects of alcohol on her already jangled mood, Imogen now grabbed for the bottle and slopped an amount of the rich red liquid into a glass, not caring that some of it splashed over the side. The thought of arriving here in this room, having come along the secret passageway, to discover Raoul entertaining his female visitor, possibly even in bed with her… She needed the wine even more at the thought, gulping it down with foolish abandon.

That would be worse…

Shocked, she pulled herself up short, the closing of her throat making it impossible to swallow the last dregs of her wine. How could it have been worse if she'd come upon Raoul here, with another woman? How could that possibly be worse than *this*? Worse than the destruction of her hopes and dreams, her plans for the future?

For both herself and Adnan.

The sudden opening of the bathroom door behind her made her start, and she almost choked on the rich liquid.

'Don't kill yourself.' Raoul's tone was dry and darkly amused. 'You're supposed to sip the stuff, not swig it down.'

'I do know how to drink wine,' Imogen managed as she forced the liquid past the knot in her throat. 'I'm not the same person you met all those years ago.'

Then, she'd rarely drunk wine, or alcohol of any sort. She'd seen what it had done to her father in his dark days and she'd never wanted to go down that road herself. But Raoul had introduced her to the sensual experience of a really good wine, the enjoyment of sipping it slowly.

Not like she'd done just now.

'I can see you're not,' was Raoul's drawled response, the dark gleam of his eyes going to the drops of wine on the table, the level in the bottle that had dropped rather too far for comfort. 'But clearly your father is.'

It was a remark guaranteed to have her slamming the near-empty glass down on the nearest surface. She had forgotten that she'd confided in Raoul the reason why she was so hesitant to share the bottle of wine he'd brought over to her table on her first night in Corsica. He had taken it that she'd been accusing him of trying to get her tiddly, so she had flung the explanation at him in a nervous rush, anxious that this devastatingly handsome man should not think her naïve or, worse, that she was trying to repulse his approach.

Short of admitting she'd been watching him for some time across the bar, and begging him to stay because he'd just made all her dreams of the perfect holiday come true when he had strolled over to speak to her, she'd blurted out the truth. That her father had a drink problem and that watching him lose himself in a bottle had made her wary. That it was only because she had left him in the care of his determined sister that she had felt able to snatch a moment of freedom and enjoy this short holiday on the beautiful island.

She'd expected that he'd laugh at her, or walk away from someone so naïve and vulnerable. Instead he'd hooked a chair out with one foot and lowered himself to sit opposite her.

'Forget the wine, then,' he'd said. 'A fruit juice—or perhaps just water. It comes from the mountain springs.'

She'd been delighted, so flattered that she'd even stumbled over asking for an orange juice, but he still hadn't laughed. And he'd stayed. Stayed and talked to her all through the evening, and late into the night, sharing a meal with her and persuading her to try some of the local dishes. He'd even paid for everything—as a welcome to the island, he'd said.

It was only later as they'd met more often and as she had got to know him—or so she'd believed—that she'd been relaxed enough to try the delicious white Vermentino and the esteemed Patrimonio red made on the island. By then she'd no longer feared he might ply her with alcohol in order to get her defences down. She'd already been deeply intoxicated just on his company alone, on the devastating sexual pull he exerted without trying.

'How much had he drunk tonight?'

So he'd noticed. It hadn't been just the memory of her past admissions that had heightened his awareness of her father's weakness.

'I'm not sure—possibly just a nightcap with Adnan after you all returned home. He was planning on an early night before the big day tomorrow…' Her voice faltered. 'Today.'

'Adnan doesn't drink.'

He shocked her with how much he knew about her fiancé. Did he also know of the tragedy that lay behind Adnan's decision?

Raoul had picked up the bottle of wine, twisting it round in his hands and almost pouring himself a glass before he obviously reconsidered and replaced it on the table beside his empty glass.

Imogen wished she'd done the same. She was still so unused to the effects of alcohol that even the one glassful she'd swallowed was already starting to affect her.

Or was that Raoul himself? It was illogical, quite the opposite of what she'd have expected, but now that Raoul had emerged from the bathroom, towel discarded and replaced by more concealing clothing—a white linen shirt and dark denim jeans—she should have felt much safer, more at ease. But the sensations that were stinging along her nerves were not calm, nor the remotest bit relaxed. Instead they were like the fizzing of an electrical current of awareness. He'd obviously splashed water on his face; the sheen of moisture still glossed his cheekbones and spiked the impossibly thick dark lashes around his eyes. Tiny crystal drops sparkled like diamonds in the jet-black strands of his hair, and the brilliant white of his shirt had been left hanging open against his tanned skin, highlighting the scattering of crisp black hair.

Dressed, but not fully. Clothes just tossed on because of her demand, but the open defiance of what she had wanted was clear in the casual half-dressed style he had adopted. It had once delighted her and made her blood heat, her heart race so fast. But that had been when she was strolling on a sunlit beach, or sitting beside the pool at the hotel, bare feet dangling in the cool blue water. It was not here, not now, not in his bedroom.

Nervously she twitched the sides of her robe close together again, then wished she hadn't, as she saw his dark eyes flick sideways to follow the betraying movement. Besides, she had no need to fuss, did she? He had already made it plain that his thoughts were on covering her up rather than taking her clothes from her.

She could feel the hot blood slide under her skin, flooding her cheeks with warmth at the thought. She could only pray that Raoul might take her response as being the effects of the rushed gulp of wine which was marking her skin as fast as the alcohol went to her head.

'So what do we need to talk about?'

She took refuge in attack and saw those straight black brows draw together in displeasure at the sharpness of her tone.

'You told Adnan the truth.'

It was obvious that was the last thing he had expected.

'That we were…'

The word 'lovers' wouldn't come. It didn't accurately describe what they had been. Sex buddies? Friends with benefits? No, not *friends*. Adnan was a friend—*had* been a friend, she adjusted painfully.

'That we'd slept together. Did you think I wouldn't?'

'I thought you might want to deny what we had.'

'What did we have? You were a holiday fling, that's all.'

The way that one black eyebrow drifted upwards, questioning her declaration, made her stumble over her words.

'So—so I wanted it to go on a bit longer towards the end—what was wrong with that?'

Crazy with love for him, she had ignored his declaration that it was only a holiday fling. She'd teased him and tried to seduce him into agreeing that she could stay. That they could stay together. Maybe even make a commitment. She hadn't been prepared for the dark storm cloud that had settled over his face; the way he had shaken off her hands.

'At the time, I *thought* I wanted it,' she flung at him. 'That didn't last long.'

Something dark slid across his face, throwing shadows into those golden eyes.

She'd more than 'wanted it to go on a bit longer', Raoul recalled. She'd been pushing to keep the relationship going when she went back to Ireland. She'd even tried to get him to ask her to stay in Corsica, to move in together. *This relationship could really be going somewhere*, she'd said.

For a brief time, he'd fallen for it. It was only when Rosalie, the daughter of family friends—and for a brief time a teenage fling—had seen that he was actually considering going along with what Imogen wanted that things had changed. She'd admitted that she'd let it drop that Raoul was not just the farmer he'd made himself out to be. Imogen's sudden change of position had come about, Rosalie had said, because she had discovered the wealth that was the reality behind the 'simple farmer' pretence. Imogen had known exactly who he was and obviously that was why she was suddenly not going to be content with the two-week time limit on their holiday affair.

That was when he'd realised he'd been taken for a fool once again. That, like other gold-diggers before her, Imogen wanted the man she'd found out he was, not the story he'd told her to act as a protective shield.

That had burned so badly that he hadn't even been able to see straight. Because he'd felt something different for her. He'd wanted—hoped—that she would be someone who wanted *him* and him alone. Not the fortune he'd hidden from her.

'I didn't know you were protecting yourself that way,' Rosalie had admitted. 'I really thought she already knew…'

Imogen knew now. Raoul could mark the change

in her from the moment his friend had let slip the truth. The girl he had thought was quiet, shy, innocent, so unlike the women who threw themselves at him with an eagerness that did nothing to conceal the gleam of greed, the euro signs in their eyes, was nothing of the sort. It had burned like acid to realise that she had only been that way as a carefully calculated approach. Once she had learned the truth from Rosalie, she had set herself to entice him in a way that was such a change around from her original behaviour that it was like a harsh slap in the face.

'And I certainly wasn't prepared to lie to Adnan. Not now. When he'd promised me so much, surely he deserved to know the truth.'

Only when he had appeared so unexpectedly, Raoul reminded himself. When he had discovered his fiancée in another man's room, another man's arms. Acid curdled in his belly at the thought she had only felt obliged to reveal the truth to her groom-to-be when circumstances had forced her into it. She had obviously not told him the full story, though. The acid ate into him more violently at the thought that, if Imogen had never admitted that they had been lovers until now, then there was no way that the other man could know about the baby.

His baby. The one she had aborted without a second thought.

Suddenly, he couldn't bear to be so close to her. The scent of her skin that he had previously found so enticing now made bile rise into his throat. The bottle of wine sent out a tempting message, offering a promise of the obliteration he had enjoyed when he had first learned what Imogen had done, but he forced himself to turn away, pacing across the worn carpet to stare out of the window into the darkness of the night.

Above the wide expanse of countryside, and the paddocks where beautiful thoroughbred horses grazed during the day, the stars glittered against the black velvet of the sky. His grandmother had once told him that the stars were the souls of tiny babies who had left the world too soon, waiting for their parents to join them. Was his son or daughter there, looking down at him and the mother who hadn't wanted their child?

He had to swallow down hard against the nausea before he could speak again.

'I thought the time for truths of that sort would have been earlier—when he asked you to marry him.'

Perhaps, if he'd been looking at her, then Imogen might not have been able to reveal the full truth. She couldn't help but feel that it put her in a position of danger to let this man know any more about the way her marriage had been arranged. The bargain she had made with Adnan.

'He didn't.'

It had been a sort of mutually accepted fact that this was how they were going to proceed—a business deal, really, but one in which they cared about each other enough to make certain aspects of it work. The memory of how it had felt to be held close to Raoul—the heat that had seared through her, then and in the past, the acknowledgement of how easy it would have been to go along with the heir-making part of *that* relationship—made her bring her teeth down sharply on her tongue to stop herself from adding anything even more stupid to her last remark.

But it was too late. Raoul had clearly already noted it, spinning round to subject her to a frighteningly intent scrutiny.

'He *didn't ask*?'

'We didn't need things like that. It was…accepted that we would marry. Almost from the day we were born.'

That was the story they'd decided on if anyone challenged their commitment. She'd never expected to have to justify it to this man who'd stolen her heart so that, like Adnan, she didn't have one to give to anyone else.

'We both grew up here, and were both likely to inherit the two studs. So joining them together through a family union seemed inevitable.'

What had she said to draw those dark, straight brows together in an ominous frown?

'And this arrangement—was it in place when we were together?' It was a harsh demand.

'Er…no. We were…' She couldn't believe she was actually going to say this. 'We were on a break.'

They'd rebelled against the way that both their families had kept suggesting that the dynastic union was the best way to go. Adnan had lost the real love of his life when the girl he had wanted to marry had been killed in a vile hit-and-run accident, and Imogen had come to feel that she could never go through with a marriage without love and passion. That was why she had been holidaying in Corsica. She'd needed the freedom and relaxation to find herself. To find what she really wanted in life.

She'd believed that in Raoul she'd found what she wanted, only to discover that he didn't want her. And he wouldn't have wanted the tiny baby she had barely realised she had conceived before she'd lost it. When she'd come back to Ireland after the nightmare of her visit to Ciara in London, she'd understood so much more about the way Adnan had felt. At the same time, it seemed that he had sensed the deep wound in her, so that his consideration, his gentleness, had made it so much easier to accept the marriage of convenience that was all he had to offer. He had never asked for details about her private sense of loss, and for that she had been grateful, knowing that to tell anyone would rip open the barely healed scar and leave it raw and bleeding.

Somehow, by opening her eyes wide and staring straight ahead, Imogen managed to force back the burn of salt behind her lids. She needed to rebuild her defences, put something up between herself and Raoul. He was getting far too close.

'And, besides, we—you—were nothing but a holiday fling.'

He hadn't liked that. She saw the blink of his heavy lids, the way his head came up.

'A holiday fling—was that all?

'Of course it was!' Did her claim sound too emphatic, too shrill? It seemed so in her ears. 'You don't think I wanted you to marry me, did you?'

His expression said everything she had thought she'd imagined back then, and she had been dreading that he might remember to throw it in her face.

'You did, didn't you!' she bluffed, grateful for the lingering effects of the wine that took the edge off the dark bruises of her memories. 'Oh, really, Raoul—sorry to disappoint you. You were fun, but you were just not that irresistible.'

He shrugged away her comment with a nonchalance that said the idea had never really troubled him, even if it had crossed his mind. Seeing that gesture, Imogen was taken right back to the beach at Rondinarra on the penultimate day of her holiday, and the way he had already been running the relationship from one step removed, distancing himself from her even before her time on Corsica was up.

'And now?' he questioned, not really sounding at all interested.

That made her determined to give it to him with both barrels. Two years ago, his indifference had almost broken her. She was not going to let him hurt her that way ever again.

'Now you've blundered in with both feet and ruined everything. There's a wedding service and reception prepared for tomorrow—today. I'm supposed to be getting married and obviously now I'm not—and that's all thanks to you. So what the hell am I supposed to do now?'

'You could always marry me.'

'Oh, now you're being ridiculous!'

She stopped, stared, unable to believe the seriousness in his face. The black humour had been bad enough. This pretence that he meant it was too much.

'You don't—' She stopped, confusion running across her features. 'Why would you want to marry me?'

A lift of those powerful shoulders dismissed her question. He obviously believed she should know exactly what was behind the crazy suggestion.

'For the same reason as Adnan would, I believe.'

'To get the stud? Believe me, it's not worth it.'

She'd blurted it out before she could think, and she realised it was a dangerous mistake as she watched his expression close up, golden eyes narrowing until they were just slits above his carved cheekbones.

'Is that why Adnan was marrying you?'

It was like the pounce of a hunting tiger, launching himself at his prey. Her stomach knotted to think of what she'd revealed. He'd accused her of being a gold-digger once and now she had obviously just confirmed his dark thoughts.

'I— Obviously, not! There was much more than that.'

Which was the truth, but only part of it.

At her side, Imogen's fingers clamped against her thigh as she fought for the control she needed. The warmth of her own skin against her hand was a stinging reminder of the way she was dressed—or, rather, undressed. Just the thought had her reaching again for the edges of her robe, jerking them together unnecessarily.

'There's no need to worry.' Raoul's lazy drawl froze her jittery fingers as they closed over the belt, wanting to tighten it as much as she could. 'Believe me, every inch of your body is hidden from prying eyes. Except perhaps your legs.'

That bronze gaze drifted down to where the red silk ended and her slender legs and feet were revealed. A carefully calculated moment of assessment and then his eyes came back up again fast, to clash with her own so fiercely she felt stars explode inside her thoughts.

'But then, I have a very good imagination—and an exceptionally long memory.'

Imogen felt as if the room had tilted wildly, and

she longed to lift her hands, to bury her burning face behind her palms, but she refused to give him the satisfaction of seeing how accurately his pointed remark had hit home.

She had never felt this nervous, this vulnerable, with Raoul in the past, even when she had been totally naked with him. Then, she had found a new and glorious sense of self-esteem to know that this stunning, powerful man who could have had his pick of any of the female holiday makers staying in the hotel had wanted her. She had been his from the start, lost in the wild fires of her first adult sexual passion. She still felt that way, just to be in the same room as him. As he'd said, she was adequately clothed, far more modestly covered than on any of the days when she had worn a bikini at the swimming pool; and yet she felt totally naked, brutally exposed, and sizzling in response to the dark power of the man on the other side of the room.

Adnan had never made her feel like this, even for a moment, she realised with a terrible sense of shock. It didn't matter that he was a gorgeous man with the honed body of a professional sportsman from his days in competitive riding. She had always only felt the warmth and closeness of their friendship. Other women had felt very differently. She'd seen it in the green-eyed jealousy that she'd caught directed at her when their engagement had been announced. She'd also seen how her own sister's eyes had widened when she'd first introduced her to her fiancé.

But the shocking, heart-twisting truth was that, when Raoul was in a room, he was the only man she was aware of.

It had been one hell of a mistake letting himself remember what she looked like under that robe, Raoul told himself, knowing that now he had remembered there was no chance of him forgetting again. Hell, as if he had needed to *remember*. The image of her tall, sexy body had been imprinted on his brain ever since those long, hot days—and even hotter nights—of the Corsican summer they had shared. He had only to close his eyes to see her again, even when they had been miles apart.

Now that they were in the same room, with the scent of her skin coiling around him, the sound of her softly accented voice in his ears, the recollection of the way it had felt to hold her close and the thunderous pounding of his heart were scrambling his thoughts. He needed to think but his body was one raw pulse of hunger, the primitive need that he hadn't felt in so long.

Not since she had walked away from him without once ever looking back. Taking the child he hadn't known she carried with her.

How could he still want such a woman? And want her with a hunger that was threatening to destroy his mind? Because his mind was not involved or, *grâce à dieu*, anything that could be described as his *heart*. He had come here telling himself that he wanted revenge for what Imogen had done to his child but standing here like this, feeling the thunder of blood at his temples, knowing that his body ached with a hunger he could barely control, he was forced to admit that there had been more to it than that.

It was about a much more primal need than he had ever been able to acknowledge until now. He still wanted Imogen O'Sullivan and he wasn't going to leave until he had her in his bed again.

He could even cope with the way his mind seemed to split in two. Hating her for what she was, what she had done, and yet knowing he had never been able to forget her. He could never go back to Corsica until he had sated himself on that glorious body that still held him in thrall, no matter how much he might wish he could resist.

CHAPTER SIX

'I HAVE TO GO...'

Imogen was looking towards the door, slender bare feet moving restlessly on the floor. He couldn't let her go, not yet. For one thing, he knew that if she turned and walked away from him he might not be able to resist the primitive urge to go after her, grab her arm and haul her back against him. If his control shattered so badly then heaven knew what would happen as a result. Or did he mean hell?

'And that's it? You just go back to your room and—what?—go to bed?'

Her shrug seemed controlled, almost resigned. He wanted more from her, wanted to see her hurt as he'd been when Pierre had told him about the child. Apparently he'd learned of it from Ciara and Pierre had enjoyed telling his brother-in-law the black truth. Even knowing that his philandering brother-in-law had flung the vile story at him in an attempt to distract him from the fact that he had still been chasing after the younger O'Sullivan sister despite her leaving his employ, Raoul had felt as if his heart had been ripped from his chest and he'd wanted her—the woman who had caused that pain—to feel the same. But now that he was face to face with her in the moment of success, the triumph he had wanted to experience wasn't there.

He was on the verge of getting everything he'd wanted out of this and yet…he'd got nothing. This wouldn't bring back the child he'd lost. The triumph he'd thought he'd feel tasted like dust in his mouth.

'What else is there to do?'

'I thought you said we needed to talk.'

'We've talked!'

At last she was showing a spark of feeling, but not in the way he'd wanted. It did nothing to ease the cold, hard lump inside where his heart should be.

'Not enough.'

An autocratic wave of his hand dismissed her protest.

'What else is there?' Imogen demanded.

'Well, for one thing, you don't seem exactly broken-hearted about Adnan's defection.'

Did he really want to think she might have *loved* the other man? Or that he had loved her? Hell, no. He wouldn't put another man through what he'd endured when she'd left him. He was damned sure that Imogen was *not* in love with Adnan.

'Of course I never wanted to hurt him. I wouldn't have done that willingly but for you. What you did tonight, *you're* the one who hurt him.'

'Hurt his pride, more likely. I saw his face when he came into the room—and I watched him last night with you. I've never seen anyone less in love.'

'You think so?' Defiance rang in her tone, and he saw the way her neat chin lifted high.

'I know so.' It was arrogant and hard. Totally assured.

She had to acknowledge that Raoul was right,

Imogen admitted unwillingly. Though she was shocked at how easily he had seen through the act that she and Adnan had put on so that everyone would believe their marriage was real. Even Ciara had been convinced. She had to have been, because Imogen knew that her sister would have tried to dissuade her from going through with the marriage if she'd thought it was fake. And she'd promised Adnan that this arrangement would look like a marriage that meant something, so she had had to keep to that promise, even if it meant pretending to her new-found sister.

It was bad enough knowing that Raoul had seen through Adnan's behaviour, but the thought that he might also have seen the truth of her own emotions made her feel as if the robe she had tightened round her so desperately only moments before was now as constricting as a corset, making it almost impossible to breathe.

'You won't exactly come out of this smelling of roses!' she flung at him, needing to attack him to hide the tsunami of feeling that was raging inside her. 'That stupid deal you came here for will all be for nothing. You don't think Adnan will want to go through with it after this!'

'Do you really think that was what I came here for?'

The challenge made her head go back, her face tensing.

'Well, it sure as hell wasn't for me.'

Again, there was that flicker of an expression across his face, changing the set of his muscles, the burn of his eyes. It made her shift uncomfortably from one foot to the other on the shabbily carpeted floor, her eyes going unwillingly to the bottle of wine and the two glasses. Surely another drink would ease this dragging, draining tension between them? But she didn't want to go that way, the way her father went when anything went wrong, the path that had contributed so much to the perilous state they were in. Would her mother have left if Joe hadn't already been too keen to turn to alcohol when times got rough? Could she and Ciara actually have shared a childhood, grown up together, if alcohol hadn't been Joe's answer to everything?

'Two...' she said unexpectedly, and saw that dark frown appear again in puzzlement at her words.

'Two?'

'Two glasses. You have that bottle of wine and two glasses.'

A sharp, silent nod was his only answer, acknowledging her awareness, but waiting for her to take the puzzle further.

So how much of this had he planned? Had he been expecting someone else here tonight? She knew he was a devastatingly good-looking man, but would he have been able to pick up another woman, met in the village only this afternoon? He'd done that with her in Corsica, so she guessed he was capable of doing exactly the same here.

'Who were you expecting?'

The devilish smile that curled up the corners of that wide, sensual mouth was warning enough. But it was a warning she knew it was too late to heed.

'I was waiting for you,' Raoul drawled, letting that smile grow, widen fiendishly.

'You...'

Just the thought knocked the air from her lungs, leaving it hard to breathe.

'You thought I would come to you!'

'Not thought.' It was a flat, dark statement. 'I knew.'

'No way.'

That she might be so easy to read was something from her nightmares. If he had guessed—known—that she would come to find him, then what else might he know simply from looking into her face; reading the truth there?

Oh, dear heaven, how much of the truth could he see?

'You couldn't know!'

'Well, you're here, aren't you?' Raoul tossed at her, soft and dangerously low. 'You're here, drinking my wine.'

Imogen felt as if a noose had been thrown around her throat, inexorably tightening with every word that Raoul let fall. He had known. He had prepared for just this, ready for her to fall into his trap.

But how could he have known? How had she given herself away? A dark thread of fear ran through her veins, making her shiver. When she thought of the devastation the evening had brought, her legs weakened, threatening to give way beneath her. How much of this had he planned?

How much of this had been just bad luck and how much had Raoul acted as the master manipulator, pulling the strings of the puppets he had under his control, making them dance to his tune when they didn't even know the name of the song?

'How could you know?'

'I know you.'

'Oh, come on, how can you claim that?' she scoffed, wincing inwardly at the high pitch that turned her defiance into a squeak of fear. He was watching so intently that she couldn't hide a thing from him. 'You knew me once, for what—two weeks, if that? We were just ships that passed in the night, a holiday fling—a lot of fun but… but…'

'But what, Imogen?' Raoul challenged with that singular, individual pronunciation of her name that only he used. The one that brought back the memories, the long, warm days of Corsica, the hot passion of the nights in his bed.

'But nothing more…'

She broke off in shock and disbelief as he shook his head so fiercely that the tiny diamond-like water droplets still lingering on his hair from his rapid face-wash scattered over her, sprinkling her face with moisture.

'How can you say nothing more? How dare you say there was nothing else between us?'

'Oh, yes, there was sex!'

High and tight, she flung the word in his shuttered face, knowing a sense of despair as she saw that there was no flicker of reaction, not even a blink of those basilisk eyes.

'And that was all.'

'All?' To her horror, it was almost laughter, the word shaking on the edge of dark amusement. 'You call that all?'

She wished she could convince herself that there had been nothing more but, watching the way his mouth moved on the words, scorched by his smile, she knew that even to describe them as old flames wouldn't come anywhere near it.

Old flames still burned and she could feel the heat searing the room, recognised the smouldering embers in Raoul's deep-set eyes.

'All…' she tried but the word was just a croak in her throat.

Raoul smiled that dark smile. Lifting one hand, he crooked a long finger, beckoning her towards him.

'Come here,' he said, unexpectedly softly.

'No.'

She wanted to shake her head in rough denial of the command but her neck seemed to have stiffened so that all she could manage was a slight tilt backwards, her chin coming up in defiance. That smile grew worryingly.

'Scared?' It was even softer, tightening the knot in her stomach.

'Scared? Never!'

Oh, but she was. And not of him. It was herself she was scared of. The fizz of electricity along her nerves, the burn of fire in her veins, made her feel as if her body was not her own. Once again the puppet master was pulling her strings and she had no choice but to dance to his tune.

He was going to kiss her, no matter what. She saw it in the darkness of his eyes, the way the black pupils had almost obliterated any trace of colour. She could see the curve at the corner of those sensual lips, the way they were slightly parted over his white teeth. She could almost taste him on her own mouth already, the memory of years ago so vivid that she expected to feel the warmth of the sun on her back, the shift of soft sand between her toes.

He was going to kiss her and she could read the thought in his face. He believed that all he had to do was move forward, take her face in his hands, lift her mouth towards his…and she would either melt into his embrace—or twist away from him and run for the door. Either one of those reactions would show him just too much of what she was feeling, however hard she tried to hide it.

That was what he expected. But there was one way she could take the initiative, knock him off-balance. He wasn't getting all his own way on this; and, right now, that one way fitted so much with what she wanted anyway.

'Not *scared*!' she declared and, high on the excitement of wrong-footing him, dodging the hand that was reaching for her, she almost danced towards him, taking him by surprise as she came close enough to drop a fleeting butterfly kiss on that warm, sensual mouth.

There, and away again…or at least that was how it was supposed to be. That was the way she'd seen it in her mind before she'd embarked on this. The kiss she'd wanted since the first moment she'd seen him again in the church, and she was allowing herself to take just this one kiss—and then she would be gone… Everything going her way, at last, nothing his.

But in the moment her lips touched his—when the taste she had recalled became real, the warmth of his skin brushing against hers, his breath mingling with her own uncontrolled gasp—she knew that she'd overplayed her hand. That she'd lost. All thought of holding back vanished in a heartbeat. One kiss was not enough, would never be enough. She couldn't just sip from that glass. Once she had tasted, she needed to drink deeply.

'Raoul…'

The sigh escaped her in the same moment that

his mouth formed her own name. Then he had moved, taken her arms, held her just where he wanted her. His dark head bent, his mouth closing over hers.

It was the gentleness that shocked her. There was no lust or demand in his kiss, nor was he holding back. Oh, dear Lord, but he was *not* holding back. His mouth took hers with a caress that seemed to draw out her soul and place it right in his hands. She had lost all sense of herself except where she ended and he began. It was as if they were just one person, two combined into one, perfectly aligned, perfectly absorbed.

Her bones seemed to melt as she leaned into him, feeling the warmth and the scent of his flesh enclose her, her breasts pressed close against his skin, which was exposed where his shirt hung open. It was like coming home, and yet it was the slow burn of a dormant ember, one that was being fanned back into life with every breath she took, every caress, every new pressure of his mouth. The slow, seductive slide of his tongue along the seam of her lips enticed her to open to him, taking in that taste, the warmth that was more intoxicating than any potent spirit sending her blood racing.

Had she kissed other men in the time they had been apart? She had to have done—there had been other guys who had tried to win her round from the pit of loneliness and darkness she'd fallen into when she had finally come home from London. There had even been Adnan…

But right now, Adnan was just a name to her. She couldn't even conjure up the image of his face, his presence. Least of all, his kisses. It was as if he had been a dream and this—this was reality. The only reality she knew. The only reality she wanted.

'Imogen…'

It was a murmur against her mouth as he adjusted his position slightly, just enough to ensure that every inch of her was pressed against him. There was still no pressure; he was so careful, so measured. That restraint was already fretting at her own control, fraying it at the edges, making her struggle with impatience, with the need for more.

His hands had curved over her shoulders, the

heat of his palms burning through the fine scarlet silk and seeming to brand her skin, to mark her out as his. As they slid slowly down her back, smoothing along her spine, she couldn't hold back the murmur of response that slipped from her as she lost all sense of control. With a little shimmy of her hips she moved closer still, feeling the hard heat of him pressed against her pelvis, noting the way his breath caught in his throat as he reacted to her enticement.

'Want…'

It was all she could manage, all she could think. She was so far gone that she didn't recognise the danger she had put herself into until she heard the faint sound of his soft laughter, felt him nod his head in dark agreement.

'I know, *ma belle. Je sais...* And this will make it so much better—easier.'

Easier? The word exploded in Imogen's thoughts. How could this be easier? Suddenly, the rush of realisation became a sense of shock and horror, despair flooding through her as she realised what she was doing, the depth of the trap into which she had fallen all over again.

She thought she'd come to terms with the gentle friendship she had for Adnan. Had told herself she could live with that and be happy. It was safer, kinder, than what she had known before with Raoul. But now there was no Adnan, there was only Raoul, and he had opened the door she had thought so firmly locked against her memories. Those memories were dragging her in and down into the same danger that she had known before.

This was how he had made her feel all those years ago, in Corsica. This was how he had swept her up into a heated world of fantasy and sensuality that had stopped her from thinking, destroyed her ability to reason. She had fallen head over heels, believing that what she felt was love—a love that he shared. Now she knew so much better. She knew all he had felt for her was the burn of lust, the stab of the most basic, primitive hunger a man feels for a woman.

It had flamed hard and hot and hungry—but only for a short time before it had burned itself out. She had still been riding high on the waves of her first encounter, with the passionate feelings that a grown woman could know, when he had tired of the whole thing and had let her drop from a very great height. She had landed so hard and so violently she had never fully recovered.

Now he had stirred up all those unwanted and unwelcome feelings all over again, making a mockery of her belief—her hope—that she was over them for good.

'Easier!'

How could this ever make anything easier between them? It just twisted things, making them infinitely more complicated than they had been in the moments before their lips had met.

That kiss had opened up her long-locked, hidden Pandora's box of sensuality and feelings and there was no way she was ever going to be able to close it again. But if Raoul thought that that made her *easy*…

She wrenched her mouth from his. She pulled away so she could stare into his face, seeing the burn of sensuality under the heavy lids, the moisture that glistened on his mouth from her foolish, unthinking kisses.

'If that's what you think then you had better

start thinking again! There's no way that anything between you and me could be any sort of easy. I wish I'd never seen you in the first place—and I *so* wish that you'd never turned up here again. If I never see you again in my life, it will be way too soon.'

The laughter that shook his powerful form had little real amusement in it. Instead it was filled with a hateful triumph that scalded her mind just to hear it.

'Forgive me if I don't believe you, *ma belle*,' he drawled softly. 'You can claim the words—but that's not what your kisses say.'

'My kisses?'

Imogen laid her hands flat against his shoulders, pushed with all the strength she could gather up and was happy to find that she must have caught him off-balance, or so sure of himself that he hadn't braced against any possible response she might make. With one sharp push she had him taking an unwary step backwards, and then another, freeing her to twist away from his grip and move partway across the room.

'You believe in my kisses Raoul?' she tossed

at him, enjoying seeing the momentary blink of confusion that flittered across his face before he caught it back and froze into immobility.

'Well, more fool you. Because kisses can deceive every bit as much as words, in fact. And I should know.'

She was almost at the door now, fingers on the handle. She couldn't get out of there fast enough, but she had one last riposte to fling at him, tossing the words into his now dark, shuttered face.

'You see, I learned how to lie with a kiss from the very best. I learned it from you.'

And that was as good an exit line as she was going to get, she told herself as she pulled the door open and dodged through it as fast as she could. She didn't dare look into the black, opaque sheen of his eyes. The way every muscle in his face tightened in anger was more than enough warning that she'd stretched what little patience he had left to its absolute limit.

'You're a great teacher, Raoul,' she tossed over her shoulder as the door began to close behind her. 'You must be if I convinced you!'

CHAPTER SEVEN

THE CHURCH LOOKED every bit as beautiful as she had hoped. But the lovely arrangements of flowers, the huge, beeswax candles, were all destined to go to waste. The wooden pews would remain empty, the candles unlit, the aisle silent throughout a day that should have been filled with the bustle and murmur of invited guests, family and friends.

No one was coming to the wedding. Not even the groom, it seemed, though she'd hoped and prayed for a reprieve. Adnan was determined to stay away and have nothing to do with what was supposed to have been their wedding day, and who could blame him? As a result, she was here alone, at this time when she should have been preparing for the big event, getting ready to put on the beautiful, elegant wedding dress that had been hanging in her wardrobe for the past few days.

She would never wear that dress now. Not even for the sort of marriage of convenience that she and Adnan had agreed on, eyes wide open, knowing that what they planned would suit them both—and help everyone else involved.

Now she couldn't even get in touch with her ex-fiancé. She didn't know where he was or what he was doing. She had tried to ring him again and again through the night and had only ever got voicemail.

'Leave a message and I'll get back to you.'

He hadn't, of course. Her own phone had remained stubbornly silent, except the one time when it had rung and it had been a call from Ciara.

Imogen shook her head as she recalled the stilted, difficult conversation with her sister. It had been like going back a couple of years to the time of their very first conversation, when her sister hadn't been too sure she wanted to meet up, to reconnect with the family she knew so little about. Imogen had thought—hoped—that they'd got past that and were on their way to creating a real family relationship. But last night had changed everything. Ciara wouldn't be here to support her through the misery of cancelling everything involved with the day. Wherever Adnan was, her sister was there with him, but the younger girl had refused to tell her where they could be found.

'He doesn't want to talk to you,' she'd said, her voice sounding strange and alien, the unusual echoes around it making it almost eerie, and totally unlike her sister's usual warm tones.

'But I have to explain to him. I'll come to the manor.'

A long pause. She could hear Ciara's breath at the other end of the line, and the silence had worried her.

'We—he's not at the manor and he won't be for some time. He's not coming back, Immi—and really, after what happened, you shouldn't expect him to.'

And then the phone had been switched off, confusing her even more. She'd assumed that Ciara had gone after Adnan last night to try to make him see reason and obviously that had failed. But…

Just what did that 'we' mean? Why was Ciara still with Adnan? And where were they?

The truth was that that last comment had had a clear note of reproof in it. A note that made Imogen realise that, even though they'd made great strides in getting to know each other after the distance their parents' split had put between them, there were still areas of her sister's life where she didn't really know Ciara at all.

'I knew I'd find you here.'

It could only be one person's voice. Only one man had those deep, slightly husky tones, that sexy, lilting accent. Immediately her spine stiffened, tension taking over every muscle.

'I came here because I wanted to be alone,' she managed from between lips that felt like wood.

'And I knew you'd say that,' he added, the tiny hint of amusement setting her teeth on edge.

'Then will you please do me a favour and leave me alone?'

'No.'

It was almost pleasant, but it was still the most determined, adamant refusal she had ever heard.

'Raoul!'

She turned to scowl at him, adopting the most determined look she could manage. But somehow it didn't work, that glare bouncing off his expressionless face with no effect. It was impossible not to think that she had hoped to face him today looking her very best, with her hair and make-up done, wearing that beautiful silk dress and her grandmother's Brussels lace veil. Instead, her worn jeans and a plain blue tee-shirt had been the only things she could think to pull on this morning, knowing most of the day was going to have to be spent cancelling things, apologising…

'Ma belle.'

'Don't!' Her hands came up in front of her face. 'I'm not your—your anything. Certainly not your…'

'Ah, but there you are wrong. You are beautiful—I've always thought that.'

Beautiful on the outside at least. Raoul had to fight with himself to keep his face from showing how the memories of the day he'd found out about her visit to the London clinic still burned in his mind. He'd been on a wild seesaw ride ever since he'd been told about it, even more since he had seen her again for the first time in years.

Here, in this little village church, where she had been supposed to marry Adnan today. That was why, when he hadn't been able to find her back at the house, and everyone had told him that she was nowhere to be found, he had known exactly where to come. Exactly where he'd find her.

'Spare me the flattery!' Imogen protested now and he couldn't help but smile at her vehemence.

But what was hiding behind that determination? It could be the effect of the shadows in the church, the pitiful light of the hazy sun shining through the stained glass windows, but she looked pale and drawn, as if she hadn't slept at all well. That was inevitable, he would have thought, after the way they had parted last night, the way her life had exploded in her face in the midnight confrontation in his room.

It was what he had aimed for; the reason he had come here in the first place—so why did it leave him with a raw sense of dissatisfaction rather than the ultimate triumph he had looked for?

'No flattery—honestly,' he reassured her. 'I never speak anything less than the truth.'

'The truth, huh?' Her chin had come up, her luscious mouth tightening in defiance. 'Then tell me the truth about why you've followed me here today. What part of "if I never see you again in my life, it will be way too soon" did you not understand? Why are you still in Ireland and not on your way back to Corsica?'

It was a question he'd been asking himself ever since he'd woken—after probably as bad a night's sleep as she'd had.

He'd intended to go. He'd planned on packing his bag as soon as he'd woken and clear out of the house, out of her life. But it was as he'd headed for the bathroom that the second and third thoughts had started to hit him.

The first was the result of seeing the belt lying on the floor on the far side of the room, close to the door. A long, thin strip of scarlet silk, it was the belt from the robe that she had tugged so tightly round her. It had obviously slipped free as she had stalked out of the door, tossing what she had clearly intended to be the last words she'd ever speak to him over her shoulder as she went.

When he had picked it up it had slithered in his hands, like a satiny snake, reminding him of how it had felt to have that silk underneath his fingertips, and the warmth of her skin beneath that. He'd resorted to the long, icy shower he'd needed earlier in the evening, but had found that it brought him no release from the intense pulse of unappeased desire that had tormented him. It had lingered all through the night, making him toss and turn until he'd woken in a tangle of sheets, his mind hazed with hunger, his body sheened in sweat. His last thought before falling into what had passed for sleep had been of Imogen, as had his first thought on waking.

'I never was very good at taking orders. And I came to see how you were doing.'

It was the truth. Well, at least it was part of it.

He knew he couldn't leave without seeing her again, without making a move to turn the hot dreams that had plagued his night into a reality. At least for as long as it took to get this burn of hunger out of his system. It was time to acknowledge that he hadn't been able to forget Imogen in the time since he had walked away from her on the beach at Rondinarra. That had been part of why he'd come to Ireland the first time, filled with dark fury after seeing that revealing photo of her and her sister in the gossip columns. Then he'd learned that her father was looking for a partner in his stud, and that had stayed him when he'd been about to rush into turning on Imogen the bitter rage he had felt at her actions. It had become a much larger part of why he'd stayed, to watch and learn, and later he'd made the approach that should have brought him here as a potential business partner.

Whoever had said that revenge was a dish best served cold had no idea how it could feel when that cold revenge was mixed with the revival of a blazing, white-hot sexual need that it seemed only Imogen could create in him.

'Well, now you can see I'm still standing.'

Imogen made her way out of the church, refusing to allow herself even one regretful glance back.

'So you can go and pack your bags—'

She broke off in shock as he shook his head firmly, the raven-black strands of his hair falling forward over his forehead. How was it possible that, wearing almost exactly the same outfit as she was dressed in—except that he had on a crisp, short-sleeved linen shirt instead of the tee-shirt she wore—he managed to look cool and even elegant when she felt like something the cat had dragged in, her hair already beginning to frizz in the muggy heat of the day.

'I'm not leaving until I know you're all right.'

Whether he knew it or not, that was a stab at the weakest point in her mental armour. Never had she felt so alone as she had this morning, the time when she should have been facing, if not the happiest day of her life, then at least the moment when so many of her worries would start to be resolved. She should have been the centre of attention, surrounded by family and friends. Instead, she found herself isolated, with no one to support her. Her father had locked himself in his room—with a large bottle of some spirit, she assumed—and Ciara was heaven knew where, with Adnan.

So, it was a bitter irony that Raoul, of all people, was the only person here offering her a shoulder to lean on.

'I take it you haven't heard from Adnan?'

'What do you expect?'

She turned to make herself walk down the path that led to Blacklands and was shocked to find that Raoul followed her, silently and closely.

'I can make my own way home!' she flashed at him, but was disconcerted to be met with the sort of disarming smile that sizzled all the way from her head to her toes inside the well-worn sandals she'd slipped on with as little care as she'd chosen the rest of her outfit that morning.

'I know you can. But, as I have to go that way myself, we might as well walk together.'

Then, just as she was cursing him for taking away her defensive argument, he knocked the ground right from under her feet by adding, 'Have you managed to get in touch with all your guests? I know you've been on the phone almost all morning.'

'Not everyone,' Imogen admitted, shuddering faintly inside at the thought of him observing her as she went through the painful process of phoning everyone on the guest list. 'Some had already started out and couldn't be contacted. I'll have to explain when they arrive.'

'Then wouldn't it be easier to have someone with you when that happens?'

Easier to have someone, yes—but not the man who had caused all this!

She had to pull herself up with the realisation that she couldn't dump all the blame on Raoul. If she had not gone to Raoul's room to try to talk to him then this wouldn't be happening… But had he really come to Blacklands solely to discuss the stud deal with her father—a deal that her father couldn't possibly have gone along with? Or had he had other plans, as she'd feared? Was this whole situation just bad luck—or was she being manipulated all the way along by Raoul?

She was going to ignore him, she resolved. She would pretend he wasn't there and maybe he would pack his bags and disappear. It took only seconds to realise that, without seeming to make any extra effort, he was keeping up with her perfectly easily, his long stride covering the ground at twice the pace of her own.

'What are you going to tell them?' he enquired now.

'That the wedding's been called off. Is there anything else I could say?'

'And are you going to stick to that unexpected new habit of yours of telling the truth?'

'What's new about it?'

She caught his indifferent shrug as he came close again. In spite of the muggy heat of the day, she felt a sudden shiver, as if the sun had just gone behind a cloud as blue eyes clashed with bronze.

'You obviously hadn't told Adnan—or your father—about us before I turned up.'

'There was no "us", not when I got home, so it was totally irrelevant.'

'Not if you were getting married.'

'So have you told anyone about me?'

'No—no one except Rosalie, but then she knew at the time.'

It had been Rosalie who had revealed to her just how much Raoul had been keeping back from her.

Use your eyes, she'd said. *Look around you. Look in the shops—in the kitchens in almost every hotel on the island!*

And Imogen had looked, seeing the distinctive labels for Cardini Olive Oil that she had been blind to before. She'd believed his story that he was a farmer, that he had olive trees on his land. That had been all. She had never dreamed that that was only a part of his fortune—that the rest came from the breeding of the small, sturdy Corsican horses that had brought him to Ireland to destroy the sense of peace she had thought she was reaching.

'And I was not getting married.'

'Still loving and leaving 'em?' Imogen tossed at him, not wanting to acknowledge the flutter of something deep in her stomach at the thought that there had been no one special in his life in the years they had been apart. But then, she'd already known that Raoul was not the marrying kind.

'Not loving,' he returned, flat-voiced. 'I'd be a fool to look for any such thing. And I was never the marrying kind. I told you that.'

He certainly had. Was she actually weak enough to let her memories make tears burn at her eyes? She blinked hard to keep them back, telling herself they were there for the baby who had had no hope of survival, not for its cold-hearted father who had never even known his child had existed.

Would he have cared? If she had done as she had planned, and managed to go back to Corsica to tell Raoul that she was pregnant before the agonising pain that had seemed to tear her in two had struck, would he have cared? Would he have insisted they marry for the sake of the child? The thought of that was somehow more unbearable than the way he had rejected her, turning his back on her at the end of their time in Corsica.

There was a heavy stone in front of her on the path and, eyes blurred, caught unawares, she almost stumbled on it. But she didn't fall because

Raoul's hand shot out, hard fingers clamping around her upper arm and hauling her back so she thumped against his chest, losing her breath in a totally different and much more disturbing way.

Weakly, foolishly, she welcomed the feeling of his strength against her. At a time when she felt so alone, so afraid of the future, she wouldn't dare to admit to herself how she longed to throw herself into that strength, feel it close around her.

He'd done that once before, in the sea off Bonifacio, when the tide had been unexpectedly rough. An uncertain swimmer at the best of times, she had been caught in a strong current and knocked off her feet. Going under the waves, with salt water stinging her eyes and water swamping her face, she had known a moment's panic. But only for a moment. Because then, strong, bronzed arms had closed around her, taking firm hold and hauling her up and out of the water. As she had soared out into the heat and brightness of the sun in the clear blue sky, she had known such a glorious sense of freedom and delight. It had been as if she was reborn, rediscovering the joy of living—and loving. It was in that moment that she had known she had fallen deeply, irrevocably in love with Raoul and that her heart would never truly be free ever again.

Not even when he had rejected her before the end of her holiday, tossing aside her weak, stumbling suggestions that maybe they could make this more than just a fling, that perhaps they could see each other again. That maybe she didn't have to go home…

Could he hear the thudding of her heart, see her uneven breathing? She could only pray that he would take it as being the result of coming close to falling. Though, from the dark gleam in those tiger eyes, she doubted it. He had looked that way when he had held her against him last night and he had made it plain that desire was all he felt. So she'd better get rid of the crazy idea that this time he might come to her rescue again.

'OK?' His voice was surprisingly low and husky on the question but she didn't dare to meet his eyes to try to read why that was so. Instead, she fixed her gaze on the spot where his white shirt was open at the neck, the pulse that beat at the base of his throat heavy and strong, and disturbingly in time with the hungry thunder of her own.

'I'm fine.'

She prayed it sounded convincing. She would have to be fine. No one was coming to her rescue like a knight on a white charger. Not Adnan and very definitely not Raoul.

'You can let me go now…'

It was even weaker to feel disappointment as he released her without hesitation, dropping her back down onto the path as if he was glad to be free of her.

But nothing could stop him following her all the way back to the stud. Because of course he had to go back there, didn't he? If he needed to pack his clothes, collect his belongings and get out of here?

The thought of him leaving was just the worst possible straw of misery to add to the list of wretchedness that had to be endured to get through the rest of the day.

CHAPTER EIGHT

IMOGEN SAGGED BACK wearily against the door frame, watching as the last car disappeared down the drive, heading for the main road and home. She let the hand she had raised to wave drop down against her side and closed her eyes for a moment against the sense of exhaustion that had almost overwhelmed her.

She couldn't give in yet; she still had more to do. Every guest had been spoken to personally, given an explanation—as close to the truth as possible—about the reasons why the wedding had been called off. Apologies—so many apologies—had been offered again and again, and now all the visitors to Blacklands had gone, the house empty except for the small army of catering staff who were packing away the food meant for the reception. The task was performed in a strange silence compared to the excited buzz of conversation that had first greeted her announcement.

After that there was only the floral arrangements, the decorations and—a bitter laugh nearly choked her—the dress to be taken from her wardrobe.

'If you let me know what you want doing with all this food, then I'll get on with it.'

The voice came from behind her, bringing her spinning round so fast she had to grab hold of the huge brass handle on the heavy oak door and keep herself upright with an effort.

'What does one do with enough food for three hundred people?' she sighed, despairing at the thought, and Raoul—because of course it was Raoul—shrugged his broad shoulders under the white shirt that was no longer quite so immaculate as it had been this morning.

He had been there with her all day. Every time she turned around, it had been to see his tall, lean figure moving silently and efficiently through the tasks that were needed to help sort out the confusion the cancelled wedding had created. She had never actually had to tell him anything; he had just seen what needed doing and got on with it, leaving her free to deal with the demands for explanations, the apologies, finding the parcels containing the wedding presents that would have to be returned.

'I should have thought to get a message to the caterers to stop them bringing it in the first place,' she sighed. But food had been the last thing on her mind. She'd been far more concerned with trying to get in touch with as many guests as possible to stop them arriving for the wedding that wasn't to be. It was only when she'd got back from the church and seen everything had been unloaded that she'd realised what a mistake she'd made.

And, once delivered, they'd adamantly refused to take it back.

'Freezer?'

'Only if you happen to have industrial-size freezers that actually work,' Imogen managed wryly. 'The ones in the kitchen have been there for the past fifteen years and they weren't the most modern or the best even then. We never got round to renewing them because…'

Because even then there hadn't been enough money to buy new ones, and the family finances had been leaking desperately ever since.

'Because no one cooked that much after my mother walked out and there was just Papa and me.'

'She took Ciara with her?'

Imogen could only nod silently. No point in denying it. Her mother's departure and her choice of daughter to take with her had been common knowledge at the time. She'd lived with the pitying looks, the swiftly hushed conversations whenever she appeared, her whole life. She was the daughter her mother hadn't wanted, and the whole village knew it.

'That knocked the stuffing out of my father and he hasn't been the same since. He'd always liked a drink before, but now…'

She thought she'd kept her voice even enough to avoid any further questioning, but as soon as she saw Raoul's black brows snap together in a dark frown she knew he was far too perceptive for that.

'Why not you?'

Only by digging her teeth down hard into the softness of her lower lip could Imogen hold back the bitterness that almost escaped her. The morning she'd woken to find that both her mother and her sister had gone, and no one could tell her where, was etched into her memory with the burn of acid. She knew why, of course, or at least she could explain it now. But how could anyone explain to a seven-year-old that her mother had wanted her younger sister—but not her?

Unable to get a word out without risking her precarious self-control, she waved a hand in a rather wild gesture that indicated the view from the door, the expanse of green fields, the stable buildings away to the side.

'The stud was not your mother's sort of thing?'

It was written all over her face so she didn't really need to answer, Raoul acknowledged inwardly. But still she nodded silently, those blue eyes cloudy and unfocused. She looked exhausted, worn out by the long day of explanations and rearrangements. Her delicate face was paler than ever, drawn tight over the fine bones, a touch of blue showing underneath where her pulse beat at her temples and the base of her neck.

It made him want to reach out and pull her towards him, to press his lips to the spot where the throb of her blood revealed the depth of her feelings. But, at the same moment, it disturbed him, and the fact that he'd even noticed it bothered him most of all.

Wasn't this why he had come here in the first place? To make sure this wedding didn't go ahead? To stop her from proving herself to be the gold-digger he had always believed her to be by marrying a wealthy man without love? The man she had chosen so soon after their relationship had fallen apart because he hadn't been prepared to be taken for a ride by any other woman.

And, into that toxic mix, he had to add the little sister who had seduced his brother-in-law and almost ruined his sister Marina's marriage, as well as the father who had tried to pull a fast one in the business deal they were supposed to have by claiming he had the stud rights to the magnificent stallion Blackjack, when in fact they would belong to Adnan and his family.

But nothing had worked quite as he'd planned since he'd arrived. So much had changed and complicated the revenge he'd determined on.

He'd never expected to find that Imogen was still as beautiful—if not more so—than he remembered. He hadn't thought the fiery pull of the sexual hunger he had felt for her would still be there, scrambling his thoughts and turning them into a molten pool of need. He hadn't expected to like Adnan Al Makthabi, or to find the sister to be so charming. And he certainly hadn't expected to feel the painful twist of an uncomfortable conscience to see Imogen now, when his plan was more than halfway to completion, with the grey marks of tiredness and strain around those shadowed eyes, etched along that gorgeous mouth.

He had certainly never anticipated that he would want to *help* the woman who had only come after him for his money, and who had cold-bloodedly got rid of his child before he had ever even known the baby existed.

'My mother was terrified of horses,' Imogen was saying now, her mouth twisting slightly on the low words. 'She never understood my father's fascination with them—or mine. So she didn't feel the connection with me that she obviously had with Ciara. Or that we thought she had. She wanted a girly girl—one who would enjoy clothes and make-up and perfumes as much as she did. And I'm sure she wanted to take her younger daughter because then she could pretend that she wasn't the age she was—knock a few years off the total. And of course she always thought Ciara was the prettier of her daughters.'

'She actually said that?'

A slow nod of her head was her silent answer.

'Then your mother was a blind fool,' Raoul growled, unable to hold back the disbelief he felt. 'Ciara is a little glamour puss, there's no doubt of that—that burnished hair, those emerald eyes, will be many men's fantasy.'

His brother-in-law's, for one thing, and look where that had led.

'But you are the real beauty in the family. You have a natural elegance and grace. Your hair—'

'Oh, don't!' Imogen broke in sharply, rawly, her voice cracking on the words. 'Please don't!'

'Why not?'

Looking into her eyes, he was astonished to see the pleading expression in their depths. It shook him rigid. Never before had he offered a woman a compliment—a heartfelt compliment like this one—only for her to react as if he had just thrown acid in her face.

'But you must know that's true,' he said, astounded. 'Your mirror must tell you it's so each time you look into it. And you must recall the way I— the way it used to be. I was knocked off-balance from the moment I saw you in that bar. I still am.'

'Oh, please, no!'

She shook her head so violently that the dark, silky strands of her hair flew out around her face, the soft essence of some shampoo she had used reaching his nostrils and tantalising them with the subtle fragrance.

'I don't want to think about that—I don't ever want to remember how you claim you felt back then.'

'Not claim—' he began, but her hand came up between them in a slicing gesture, cutting off what he had been about to say.

'No! The past is the past and I want it to stay there. We don't want to revive any of those unwanted memories.'

'Speak for yourself.'

He'd revive everything right this minute if he could. Nothing of the way he had felt about her had been buried. He still hungered; his body still burned for hers. The only thing that would be different was that this time…

He couldn't hold back the cynical laugh that escaped him at the thought that last time he had hated the fact that she had only wanted him for his money. This time that fact would be an advantage, a lever to get exactly what he wanted.

'What's so funny?'

'The idea of you claiming that all of that was buried when you know it's a lie. Remember…' he reproved when her pretty mouth opened, obviously about to frame a tart protest.

He found he actually liked the thought of her protesting. He didn't want too easy a conquest; a spirited woman was much more satisfying. He had enjoyed Imogen's spirit when they had been together before.

'Remember, I had you in my arms last night. I held you against me.'

The fluttering of those long, lush eyelashes told him he'd hit home with that and she was, even now, remembering just how it had felt to be that close.

'I kissed you. I felt your response—the instinctive response you couldn't hide.'

'I…'

Was she going to try to refute it? How could she even think of lying about that? He'd held her, kissed her, tasted her, felt her response. And he had known then that he could not walk away again without experiencing the heat of her embrace; the warm, welcoming moisture at the core of her; the pressure of her body against his; her slender, soft legs entwined around him, hips opening to him, breasts crushed against his chest.

Under the force of his reproving stare, she bit the words back. He could see the rapid adjustment of her thoughts, the change that flitted behind her eyes.

'You said that would make things easier,' she muttered, with a defiance that didn't match her expression. 'What did you mean by that? Make what easier?'

Now was not the time to go into that. That would come when they had time really to talk. When everything about this abandoned wedding had been cleared away. When she was left to face the future without it.

Then he would tell her what he had planned—and how she fitted into it. He would reveal most of his thoughts, but not all of them. The last truth would come when he knew he had her where he wanted her.

'Not now.'

He was already turning away, back into the big dining hall where the caterers had just about completed their packing away, and the fine food and elegant dishes were all waiting to be disposed of like so many guilty secrets.

'We have to get things sorted out. What do you want doing with all this?'

As he expected, drawing attention to all that needed to be done immediately distracted her. He actually felt a twist of sympathy when he saw the way her face paled, her eyes dulling as she surveyed the task before her. She looked very slender, almost delicate, and disturbingly vulnerable. The way she straightened her spine, squaring her shoulders, brought a new sensation of admiration for the way she was handling this. Alone.

'Where the hell is the rest of your family?' That sister—her father?

Her soft mouth actually twisted into a sort of wry amusement.

'My father will still be sleeping off his hangover or…'

A quick glance at the watch and another wry smile.

'Starting on a new one. And Ciara? You tell me. Ciara is wherever Adnan can be found, but Adnan seems to have disappeared off the face of the earth. He's not answering his phone; no one at the Hall has seen him. Not even his mother.'

'She spoke to you?' Raoul let his surprise show.

'Not for long,' Imogen admitted. 'Just to say that she had seen or heard nothing of Adnan—then she took great delight in shutting the door in my face.' Her shrug was one of resigned acceptance. 'And who could blame her? She'd been looking forward to being mother of the groom at the perfect society wedding. Watching her son make a brilliant dynastic union…'

She couldn't finish the sentence. Couldn't add the other parts of the bargain she and Adnan had come up with between them. Geraldine Al Makthabi had also been hoping to become a grandmother—and her future father-in-law to achieving his dream of becoming a great-grandfather. Under the cover of the piles of food containers stacked up on the tables, she slipped a hand over her lower belly, remembering how it had felt to think that a new life was forming there, nestling deep inside…

A new life fathered by the man who now stood beside her, amongst the ashes of her hopes. The man who had sent her dreams toppling down into ruins.

'What am I going to do with all this?' she said again, sharper now, the fight against the bitterness of her memories making her tone harsher than she had planned.

Obviously Raoul thought so too because he shot her a quick, assessing glance from under hooded lids, then those golden eyes slid away from her and a frown creased the space between his brows as he considered the food problem thoughtfully.

'Do you have an old people's care home nearby? Disabled living? A children's home?'

Impossibly, now, when she had coped with everything else that had gone before—had coped without a single tear—the introduction of a very practical solution almost demolished the walls she had built around herself. The room blurred, her eyes stung and roughly she rubbed her hands against them to dash away any tears before they even had the chance to fall.

'Great idea,' she managed gruffly. 'Perfect.'

'Leave it to me,' Raoul said and helplessly she found that she was capable of nothing more than nodding as she handed the responsibility over to him.

CHAPTER NINE

'COME AND SIT DOWN. You've been on your feet all day.'

Raoul's voice caught Imogen by surprise as she wandered into the shabby, old-fashioned sitting room where the glow of the setting sun gilded the windows and made the cream-painted walls look as if they were blazing red and gold.

'I thought you'd gone.'

She hesitated on the threshold of the room as she tried to decide whether to go in or to make some hastily concocted excuse to take her away from there, away from him.

'Not yet,' Raoul said now. 'Only just got everything sorted and finished. I helped myself to a drink. I hope you don't mind.'

He lifted a glass of white wine, so much paler than the rich, red liquid from the previous night. But still, the memory of that time in his room, the way it had trapped her with him, destroying all her plans and hopes for the future, kept her frozen, not knowing which way to move. To turn and walk away seemed impossibly rude after he had spent so much of the day helping her sort out the results of the disaster that was supposed to have been her wedding day, but to walk into the golden shadows of the room where he sprawled comfortably in a huge armchair seemed to bring an intimacy that she shied away from nervously.

'Of course not,' she managed unevenly. 'A drink's the least I owe you after the help you've given me today.'

Whenever she had needed help, whatever had wanted doing, he'd been there, silent, strong and disturbingly reliable. So now, if it wasn't for the fact that the downstairs part of the house still looked like a display for the Chelsea flower show, one might almost believe that today had never been planned as anything special.

It hadn't been anything truly special, she couldn't help reflecting, remembering the way she had been thinking in the church when Raoul had suddenly reappeared in her life. Was it really just two days before? It felt as though she had lived through several different lifetimes since then—one of them as Adnan's fiancée, another as the bride jilted almost at the altar. Or wouldn't everyone really think that she had jilted Adnan when he had found her *in flagrante* with Raoul? And now…

What was she now? *Who* was she now? What sort of life was she to go forward into when everything she had hoped and dreamed of had been blasted apart, shattered into tiny, irreparable fragments? She had seen the hope of marriage to Adnan, the joining of their two families, the restoration of the Blacklands stud's fortunes, the hope of a child to ease the non-stop nag of loss ever since she'd miscarried Raoul's baby, as a way to give herself the prospect of a future. A future that would help heal the wounds that Raoul Cardini had inflicted on her vulnerable heart.

But now that future had been closed off to her, the darkness of the bleak tomorrow she faced closing in around her. Once again, it seemed that Raoul Cardini was the darkness at the centre of the storm surrounding her that had ruined every chance of happiness. Even knowing that, when she heard him speak with quiet consideration after a day of so much anger, disappointment and upset, it was almost more than she could take.

She couldn't let herself rely on him—on anything about him. Not just for today but for any sort of future. The weakness in her heart because he had been there for her during such a difficult day was just that—a weakness she couldn't afford to indulge. She'd been here before and had paid a terrible price for her naïve trust.

'Then share it with me.'

His smile was what did it. She needed that smile, needed some company—even *his* company.

No, Imogen admitted as she moved to sit opposite him on the other side of the huge inglenook fireplace: *especially* his company. He had only been back in her life for what? Three days? And once again she was back in the feeling that had overwhelmed her from the first day of their meeting two years before. The feeling that he was as vital to her as breathing, essential to life itself. He kept her heart beating. It couldn't be for long but she would take whatever she could and be grateful for that.

She was no longer the naïve young girl who had met him in a bar in Corsica. She had much more experience of life. She had known love and loss—too much loss. She had been a mother, if only for a few weeks. She'd lost the love of her life.

There, she could finally admit that to herself as she looked into his face, the burn of the setting sun casting deep shadows across his carved features. Did she need any more evidence of what she'd known already? The loss of the wedding she'd planned with Adnan, the hopes she'd had for a future, had all but knocked her flat. But with Raoul at her side, for today at least, she'd been able to cope. His quiet strength had seen her through the day, bringing her through the rough waters of shock and distress to this quiet mooring where at least she had a moment to breathe, to let her shoulders down and to think about which way to turn next.

The idea of any time, any space, with Raoul being considered quiet or calm was such a shock that Imogen found her hand shook as she held out her glass for him to pour the wine. Since the moment he had walked back into her life just days ago, she had been in turmoil. How could she feel peace when he was the cause of all the upheaval and destruction from the start?

But she'd take it, such as it was; it was what she needed right now. And if by midnight she found that, like Cinderella, all the magic of the moment vanished and her fantasy handsome prince had turned back into a rat, then at least she would have had tonight.

'Have you heard from Ciara?' he was asking now, and only someone as attuned to everything about him would have noticed the tiny hesitation before the name. The one that revealed he had actually meant to ask had she heard from Adnan, but had held back. Was that because, like her, he wanted to enjoy the moment of truce between them, even if it was temporary?

'Not a word.'

Her tone was low, regretful, and it made Raoul scowl darkly to hear it.

'What sort of a sister is she?'

'Oh, don't!'

Imogen's head came up sharply, the wine glass jerking in her hand. The raw note in her voice, an unexpected sheen on her eyes, caught on something uncomfortable deep inside him and stilled the cynical comment he had been about to make.

'Why not? She's your sister. Family matters. I know I would do anything for my sister.'

It was part of what had brought him here after all. The way Ciara had behaved with *his* sister's husband. And because…

For a moment his vision dimmed as he recalled the photograph he had seen in the newspaper. The way Imogen had been leaning on her sister's shoulder. The slightly glassy smiles they had shared.

The Scandalous O'Sullivan sisters.

'Not for very long,' Imogen said now. 'We barely know each other.'

Raoul froze with his glass halfway to his lips again and then lowered it slowly to rest on the wide arm of the chair.

'Why not? I know your mother took Ciara with her when she left, but surely… No?' he questioned as she shook her head slowly, black hair falling loose from the tie she had it fastened with at the back, tumbling around a face that he could now see was pale and shadowed with stress.

'If you're trying to say that surely we were still sisters—well, of course we were, but we never got to see each other.'

'Never?'

Raoul became aware of the way his grip had loosened on the stem of his wine glass so that it almost tipped over. Hastily he closed his fingers round it, pulling it back, but still a small spill of wine slipped over the edge and onto the furniture.

'Pardon...' He pulled a handkerchief from his pocket and dabbed it on the offending stain.

'Oh, don't worry.'

Imogen's smile was reassuring, though slightly weary, and to his consternation he found that caught on his over-tight nerves, leaving him feeling uncomfortable and unsettled.

'That chair—the whole suite—is so old it's practically vintage. In fact, I think it was the same sofa that was in this room when my mother took off with her lover. Papa could never bring himself to replace it. In fact…'

One long-fingered hand moved over the well-worn velvet, smoothing the nap one way and then stroking it back the other way.

'He used to say he could remember his two little girls playing together on it.'

'Two little girls,' Raoul echoed, crumpling the white cotton into his hands and clenching his fingers tight over it.

That gleam in her eye was stronger, brighter. Tears? Now? Why tears for this when she had been so strong through all the rest of the day? The shift from the admiration he'd felt to a disturbing twist of sympathy was not an easy one.

'How old were you when your mother walked out?'

'Seven.' And already crazy about the horses, lost in the world of the stud, the beautiful animals bred there. 'Ciara was not quite three.'

The memory of the day she had woken up to find that not only her mother but also her beloved little sister had disappeared into the night was almost more than she could take. As she had grown up, she had tried so hard to keep this home for herself and her father—and now that Ciara had returned to the family, that had been so much more important. But Ciara had vanished, allying herself with Adnan, and the house and stud would soon belong to someone else. So what had alienated her sister?

'I know what it's like to live without a mother,' Raoul stated now, and her startled glance into his face caught the burn of darkness in his hooded eyes. 'My mother died of cancer when I was nine.'

'That must have been so horrible for you. At least I had had the chance that my mother might come back one day. You had no such hope. How on earth did you cope?'

'My father was determined to help us through. He was always there for us—and my older sister took on the mothering role as well as she could.'

'I would have loved to do that for Ciara.'

The unevenness in her voice was put there by the thought of him as child of nine. Her own memories told her how he must have felt.

'Mother kept us apart,' she forced herself to

continue, staring wide-eyed into the empty fireplace. 'We didn't even know where she was. She was determined that we wouldn't have any contact with each other—or Ciara with my father. It was her way of getting back at my father, of carrying on the civil war between them.'

'To keep sisters from knowing each other?' His disgust showed through the question, sharpening the bitterness of memory so that she had to swallow hard as she nodded her answer.

'We only found each other again a couple of years ago. We'd both been searching, but Mother had changed her name, and she gave Ciara no reference to the past—she only had the vaguest memories of a young child. It was just after we...'

The childhood memories had been bad enough but the way her reunion with her sister had coincided with the end of her time with Raoul threatened to destroy her. Lifting her head to look into his face, she saw the shadows of memory shift across his face, watched that sexy mouth tighten, as if to hold something back.

'I'd been trying to find Ciara for ages, but got nowhere.'

Focusing on that aspect of the time after she'd left Corsica gave her enough strength to tell the story without going back over more difficult memories. It had been as a reprieve from the worries of the situation at home, the frustration of finding nothing about her missing sister, that she had treated herself to the short holiday in Corsica. If only she had known she had been jumping out of the frying pan and deep into the heart of the fire when she'd done that.

'But when the financial settlement was finalised, there was no more war to fight, so my mother finally put us in contact with each other.'

She had barely been back home from Corsica before a wary Ciara had contacted her. She had barely realised she was pregnant before she had made that trip to London to meet with her long-lost sister; barely started to discover the new and wonderful experience of having a family before the tiny seed of what could have been her family for the future had been lost in the most horrific circumstances.

Recalling the shock and the pain, both emotional and physical, of those days, Imogen folded her arms around herself, cradling her lower abdomen where the minute beginnings of her baby—hers and Raoul's child—had once nestled, safe and secure. At least, it was supposed to have been safe, but fate had dealt them a brutal blow, dragging her baby from her womb and almost killing its mother in the process.

'Imogen...'

It was only when she heard Raoul's voice, the note of surprise and shock roughening its edges, that she realised that she hadn't been able to hold back the tears her memories had stirred. They were spilling down her cheeks in a silent declaration of the misery she couldn't even begin to voice aloud.

'Here.'

When had he moved? She hadn't heard a sound, or noticed any change in his position, but suddenly he was beside her, perched on the arm of the chair, reaching out to her. If he touched her then she would collapse. But no, he was holding something out to her. A blur of white through tear-strained eyes—the handkerchief with which he had wiped the wine from the chair.

'It's a little marked—not exactly the crisp white handkerchief of a regency novel.'

His voice had a surprising shake to it. Was that because he was laughing at the image—at himself?

'No problem,' she managed, breaking off as the soft cotton touched her face, pressing gently, mopping up the trails of tears down her cheeks. Her heart thudded once, hard and high up under her breastbone, making her catch her breath, and she could find no way to say anything more.

The white handkerchief smelled of his skin after it had been crushed in his hand, the traces of his personal scent still lingering. It was all she could do not to turn her face further into it, inhale that scent, take it deep into her. She wanted to lift her hand, press it against the fingers that held the cotton, crush them against her face so she could remember how it had felt to have him hold her, comfort her.

She could feel the warmth of his body next to hers, the weight of his arm around her shoulder. She'd longed for him to hold her like this in the long, dark days after she'd lost their baby. She'd even thought about contacting him again, or perhaps daring to travel to Corsica to find him and tell him what had happened. Surely at least sharing the loss and the sorrow with him would have helped.

But of course she hadn't gone. She'd felt she could never return to him, never confront him with that terrible news. Never force him to comfort her when he hadn't wanted the baby, hadn't even thought it might exist. He had never even wanted her, so how could he have shown comfort for a loss that only she had known? If she'd told him then he would have made the effort, she had no doubt. He might have expressed a degree of sorrow but it would never have been truly meant and she would have seen the effort he was making in his face, hear it in his words. She would have been broken even further by the insincerity beneath his actions.

'Your mother must have been the worst kind of person to do that to her children. I can see how it meant so much to you to meet up with Ciara again. You'll have had a lot of catching up to do.'

There was an uneven delivery to his speech,

and the pressure of his hand had altered. He now held the handkerchief still in one place, resting against her cheek, his thoughts seeming to be elsewhere.

'My sister and I are very close,' he said slowly. 'I would do anything for her.'

What had put that darker note into his words? Imogen couldn't even begin to guess. She could barely cope with the fact that he thought her sorrow was all about her family, her mother's behaviour and Ciara's. She couldn't let him in on the truth. On the fact that it had been at that special moment of reunion with Ciara that the deepest, harshest blow had hit her and it was only because her sister had been there that she had got through it.

She had even let Ciara persuade her to go out on the town way too soon, in a desperate attempt to put the sorrow behind her. Ciara too had been in an emotional state, because of the circumstances in which she'd lost her job, and they had both struggled to accept the way their mother had behaved. The glass of wine they had intended to share that night had turned into another—a bottle—and, totally unprepared for the effects of the alcohol on their systems, they had both staggered out to find a taxi before the evening disintegrated any further.

Now even Ciara had left her life, it seemed, alienated by something she didn't understand in her relationship with Adnan.

'Imogen…'

Raoul had moved, sliding down to the floor in front of her, kneeling to take her in his arms.

'Where is your father? Shall I fetch—?'

'Oh, no!'

She shook her head. The addition of her father into this emotional mix would be a move too far.

'He'd be no use at all—he's given up already and gone to bed.' With a bottle, she had no doubt. Perhaps, in a way, seeing Raoul's obvious impatience with her father's behaviour, she began to understand her mother's attitude just a little better, to see there might have been two sides to their disastrous marriage.

'Given up on what? He hasn't done a thing all day. Couldn't he have offered to help at least?'

'It's his idea of a nightmare, what happened here today.'

'And not yours?

She hadn't expected his anger, and that sceptical glance, the narrowing of those penetrating eyes, was too much, too close. Hastily she tried for a diversion in the hope of distracting him.

'He looked in once and saw you were there.'

She'd seen her father put his head round the door and back away at the sight of Raoul in full organising mode.

'I suppose he saw that I had some clothes on.' The twist to Raoul's mouth was wry. 'And that was enough.'

Laughter choked in Imogen's throat at the memory of her father's awkward command in the middle of the night.

'He also heard your nickname being bandied about,' she managed, recalling the way several of the village matrons brought in to serve at the wedding breakfast, and now entrusted with the clearing up, had looked as if their eyes were out on stalks at the sight of Raoul, sleeves rolled up to expose tanned forearms as he hefted bundles of starched linen tablecloths or the boxes packed with food to go to the hospice. His hair had tumbled forward over his wide brow and he had had the look of the untamed bandit the scandal papers had named him.

'The Corsican Bandit?' A lift of his broad shoulders dismissed the familiar title. 'I've heard worse. And considering the stories that have been spreading…'

'Stories?' Imogen sat forward sharply. 'What stories?'

Those gleaming eyes clashed with her uneasy ones for a moment, then again that inscrutable smile flickered across his mouth.

'That I'm here to break your father down—to steal the stud—and worse. I think you'd better be prepared for the fact that now I'm also supposed to be planning to steal away his daughter.'

'Oh, no, they can't think that?'

The way one black, straight brow drifted upwards, questioning her assertion, had her thinking backwards, remembering the knowing looks that she'd received as she'd struggled to explain that the wedding was off, that her prospective groom had left the area—maybe even the country for all she knew.

'Would it be so very bad?'

His voice had lowered, becoming richer and darker. The soft traces of his accent had deepened, turning his words into a husky purr. The warmth of his breath told her that he was closer, his face almost touching hers. If she blinked she felt her lashes brush across his cheek, and she inhaled his intensely personal scent with every indrawn breath. The handkerchief slipped to the floor and its pressure on her cheek was replaced by the burning touch of his hand, skin against skin. She had only to turn her head and…

'Oui…'

She heard the agreement forced from his lips, felt it against her cheek as her mouth found the skin of his palm. The scent of his body was like a drug reaching straight for what little was left of her functioning brain and blotting out rational thought.

'That's what I've wanted to do all day,' she murmured as she let her tongue slide out to taste him, taking that essence of him into her mouth.

'And I've wanted that for days too.'

His voice was thick and raw, the words struggling to be heard above the beat of his heart so close to hers, the heat of his breath dancing over her skin.

'Ever since I arrived in that church and saw you there.'

'Really?'

It was all she could manage as she tried to look into his face, to read the truth in his eyes. But she found that the heat and focus of his stare was too much, too strong for her to take without dissolving into a puddle of molten awareness. Her need for him was like a throbbing pulse all along her body, centring at the juncture of her thighs. The stinging hunger that pooled there made her shift uncomfortably on the chair, uncontrollable need making her reach for him, link her hands behind his head, pulling his face down towards her, holding it there while her lips explored his with the yearning she couldn't control.

'Vraiment.'

It sounded like the truth he'd declared it to be. It sounded like the words she'd heard him whisper in the darkness of the long, hot nights on the island in the days when she knew she'd been falling in love with him. In the time when she'd thought there was no reason not to fall in love with him.

'Me too…' There was no point in denying it, so why even try. 'That's the way I've felt too. From the moment I turned and saw you.'

No, before that. As soon as she'd heard his voice and known who was behind her. Wasn't the truth that in that single moment she had known the wedding could never go ahead? Wasn't that why she had gone to Raoul's room in the middle of the night? She'd gone about things the wrong way. She should have spoken to Adnan first. She should have told him that she could never love him as he deserved a wife to love him. She should have acknowledged to herself that she had always loved Raoul, falling for him in a heart-beat and never escaping again. She'd known she could never have a proper marriage with Adnan, but that had done nothing to destroy all the reasons why she *had* to marry him and live up to their agreement.

'W-what did you come back for?' She asked and felt his soft laughter against her ear. His warmth surrounded her, cutting out the rest of the world and enclosing her in a bubble of security, if only for these moments.

'Exactly as they said,' he murmured. 'I came to steal you away.'

She didn't believe him for a moment, but right now it was what she wanted to hear. What she wanted to feel. That someone thought she was special. That she was wanted for herself, not for what she could offer him or what she brought with her.

That she was *wanted*—for this one night at least.

'I hoped that was what you'd say.'

At least that was what she had meant to say, but she barely got the first sound out before her lips were taken in a fierce, demanding kiss. Her head fell back under the pressure of his mouth, her lips opening eagerly to his plundering tongue. His long body came up and over hers, crushing her back into the chair as his heavy, muscular legs slid between her denim-clad limbs. His hands seemed to be everywhere, holding her, hot fingers pushed into her hair, the hard weight of his palm against her thigh, her hip, sliding under the hem of her top, searing across her skin. Instinctively she writhed in delight, pressing herself further into his touch, her pelvis shifting against his, pressing up against the heat and hardness of his erection, dragging a moan from him that sounded right into her open mouth.

'Raoul…' She tasted him on the breath that had filled her mouth, felt it burn all the way down to her soul. She wanted this. Oh, dear heaven, but she wanted it.

She was sliding down deeper into the chair, almost to the floor, the heat and the weight of his body against her. And it was all too much. Too hard, too hot, too heavy. And she was too hungry, too needy to take this—just this—and nothing more.

She wanted him on top of her, covering her, the hard weight of him pressing her down into the worn and shabby rug before the fire. But when he was there, sliding over her, long legs entangling with hers, it wasn't enough. He had too many clothes on and so did she. She didn't want to feel the linen of his shirt, the fine material of his trousers rubbing against her, making the denim scrape against the highly sensitised nerves under her skin.

Her hands were moving over him feverishly, tugging at the buttons in his shirt, fingers sliding in through the spaces she had made, electrical prickles of response buzzing along her nerves as she felt the crisp brush of hair against her fingertips, the heated satin of his skin.

'*Ma belle*... Imogen.'

There it was again, the sound of her name as only he could pronounce it, muttered against the arched lines of her neck, moving down, down towards where the curves of her breasts just showed above the deep vee neck of her shirt. The movement crushed the softness of her body against the hardness of his. So close—and yet far too far away. She wanted, *needed*, so much more.

But even as Raoul followed her down onto the floor, she felt the sudden tension in him, the slight drawing away from her, creating a gap between the burn of their bodies that let a disturbing drift of cooler air creep over her exposed skin.

'*Ton père*—your papa.'

Raoul could have cursed himself for the muttered words that seemed to jolt her out of the burning response she'd shown, freezing the hands that clutched at his shoulders, forcing open those beautiful eyes. Eyes that even in the dim light of the gathering dusk he could see were still glazed with passion. The last thing he wanted was to destroy the mood that had flared so fast and so hot in the moment she had turned her head to kiss his hand. But he had no desire at all to have their passion interrupted by the appearance of her father—drunk or sober. Once had been enough.

'Your room…'

It was on the other side of the house, up a separate flight of stairs. It would be silent and secret and would give them all the time in the world to give in to the sexual tension that had been burning between them since the first moment they had seen each other again, complete the connection that had never been destroyed by their separation. It had only ebbed temporarily, fading down to smouldering embers, needing the hint of a breath, a touch, a kiss, to coax it into an untamed fire that swept through them all over again, devouring every hesitation or doubt in its path.

This was what had always been between them, how he had always felt about this woman. And everything he had thought had destroyed it, the distance he had believed he had wanted to put between them, had only been a lie. This was why he had never been able to forget Imogen, why he had never been able to replace her in his thoughts, in his dreams, with any other woman. No matter how he'd tried.

And he'd tried, damn it! Tried and failed completely. So tonight was what he had been dreaming of for all the empty years since he'd walked away from her. It was all he had wanted in the time they'd been apart. And nothing—*nothing*—was going to stop it now.

Imogen was of the same mind, it seemed. He had barely whispered his warning before she was scrambling to her feet, reaching out for his hand to curl her fingers tight around his, tugging him towards the door.

'My room,' she agreed, and the thickness of her voice, the unevenness of her breathing, told him she would have as much trouble as he would to get up the stairs without ripping clothes off and discarding them along the way.

CHAPTER TEN

THEY MADE IT to the bedroom, but only just. Imogen's tee-shirt was already ripped at the seams, coming apart in Raoul's urgent hands. His belt had been tugged free, the button on his jeans snapped open in a struggle that was then abandoned in place of an assault on the fastenings of his shirt which Imogen found easier to wrench out of the way.

Small white buttons flew across the room, to land with a faint sound against the wall. The sight and scent of his skin, the temptation of the bronzed satin before her, was almost too much and she pressed her mouth against the wall of his chest, tasting and tantalising without restraint.

'Imogen…' Raoul growled, hard hands clenching in her hair, seemingly undecided whether to hold her there or to pull her head up and away so he could crush his own kisses on her hungry mouth.

The kisses he needed to give her won the battle and she found her head was pulled up, lips crushed beneath his marauding mouth, his invading tongue plunging into the moist softness, setting up a sensual dance as he tasted her intimately.

His hands were urgent at her waist, lifting the torn tee-shirt and wrenching it over her head, pausing only for the time it took to remove it before he claimed her lips again. Imogen had the easier task and with Raoul's help his shirt was soon shrugged off and tossed to one side on the floor. The white cotton bra shared the same fate, discarded without a second thought, and Imogen could only sigh out her relief and satisfaction as she felt her skin press against his, the whirl of black hair tantalising and teasing her already sensitive nipples.

'*Mon Dieu*, but I want you!' Raoul muttered roughly, pushing his hands up between them to capture and cup the curves of her breasts, teasing the sensitive nipples until she was swooning with desire, swaying against him, only supported by the hands she had flung up around his neck, fingers clenching over his shoulders, digging in to the corded muscle there.

'Me too.'

It was all she could manage, because to say anything more would require her to separate her lips from his demanding mouth and that was more than she could stand. Stinging pulses of desire were shooting through her, all the way from her nipples down to where the hot moisture of need gathered between her thighs. She was blind, deaf and dumb to anything but Raoul and the needs he was waking in her, the pleasures she knew were waiting for her, if she could just…

'These have to go.'

Sensing her needs, Raoul had already unzipped her jeans, tossing her down on the bed with an impatience that spoke of the hunger that was building up inside him too, threatening to break through the dam of restraint he had tried to impose on his actions.

And that was fine with Imogen. Patience and restraint were not what she wanted from him. Not here. Not now. Almost frantically she wriggled herself free of the clinging clothing, knowing a hot rush of relief and anticipation as Raoul's demanding hands exposed her to his hungry gaze, the faint wash of cooler air an almost unbearable addition to the rush of sensations.

'You too.'

Their hands met and clashed as both of them tried to rid him of what little was left of his clothing, and a moment later they were back down on the bed together. Imogen's arms went up around his neck as she pulled him down to cover her, giving herself up to the delicious sensation of having his hard body over hers. His hot skin scorched her, his hair-roughened legs came between hers, nudging her limbs apart, exposing her to him. All the time his mouth was at her breasts, licking, suckling, nipping sharply, until she arched high against him, letting out a high, keening cry of delight and need.

Drifting, lost on a heated sea of sensation, she felt his fingers at her moist core, brushing aside the damp curls, stroking just where she needed him most. It was too much, though, and she caught his hands in hers, demanding more.

'You,' she said roughly. 'I want you. All of you.'

His faint groan told her that he was as close to losing himself as she was, and she let her legs part even further to encourage him, inviting him in. The blunt heat of him was nudging at her; his mouth was fixed on one breast, tugging sharply on the aroused nipple as she gave herself up to his intimate invasion. Abandoning all control, she raised her hips from the bed, pushing herself against him, and felt the hard force of his possession surging into her, taking her out of herself and into a mindless, needy hunger that could only be satisfied by joining together harder and faster.

'Ma belle...'

His voice was a rough, hoarse gasp as he pushed in, deeper, further, then drew back, again and again and again. Each time he took her higher, further, the storm of pleasure building, swirling, growing until there was nowhere else to go but over the edge and into the oblivion of ecstasy that splintered all around her.

A thudding heartbeat later, she heard Raoul's

cry as he abandoned himself to his own release and followed her into the raging darkness.

It was a long, long time before her breathing slowed, her heart stopped racing and she slowly, dazedly came back to reality and awareness of the room she was in, the man who lay beside her, long body slick with sweat and the aftershocks of reaction.

'And you wondered why there are the rumours that I'm here to steal you away.'

His broad chest was still heaving, his words coming roughly and unevenly.

'I think it's a little late to try and deny that now.'

'But I can't have people thinking that—it would ruin everything.' The words escaped in an unthinking rush.

'Ruin?'

Raoul heaved himself up onto the pillow, propping it behind his back as he leaned against the bedhead.

'That seems to be a word that's been used a lot today. If I'm supposed to have ruined everything, at least you could have the courtesy to tell me exactly how I've done that.'

The way he looked down at her, the laser probe of those bronze eyes, made her shiver inside. She wanted to reach for the sheet, to pull it up to cover herself from that searching stare.

'It doesn't matter,' she hedged. 'Nothing matters now—everything's…'

'Ruined?' he supplied sardonically when she let the sentence trail off unfinished. It was unfinishable. There was nothing left to say. 'Explain!'

'Nothing to explain.'

She couldn't meet his eyes, so instead stared down at her own fingers where they lay on the bedspread, watching them trace out the pattern of the golden flowers as if they could wipe away the design and everything that had happened in the past few days. She couldn't explain anything, least of all how she had ended what had been supposed to be her wedding day here, in bed, with a man who was not the bridegroom. She had just made hot, passionate…

No; her mind flinched desperately away from the word 'love' in that sentence. She had just had hot, passionate *sex* with the man who was responsible for breaking up the marriage she had thought she would be consummating tonight.

'You can't expect me to believe that.'

'Can't expect you to believe that, because of the way you broke up my marriage plans, I am probably—no, definitely—currently spending one of my last nights ever in Blacklands?'

The full horror of the truth broke over her like a cold wave, and even the way Raoul's black brows snapped together in a fierce frown couldn't stop her.

'Can't expect you to believe that as soon as the news about the cancelled wedding gets out—which I expect it already has—there will be a line of creditors queuing up outside that door?'

A wild gesture with her arm indicated the window and the drive up to the house that lay beyond it, yet Raoul's eyes didn't follow it, but instead stayed, unblinking and fixed on her face.

'And why would they do that?'

'Because we owe them. We owe them more than we can ever pay. Even our famed stud horse isn't ours! And as soon as they see our last chance of redemption has gone then…'

'Al Makthabi was your last chance?'

He fired the question at her like a bullet and she winced as she felt it hit home.

'Yes.' Her voice was low and despondent, the slow nod of her head a sign of surrender.

'Your father has let the stud go to rack and ruin.'

His mouth twisted on the repetition of that emotive word.

'He's never been able to resist a bet—and when he had the knowledge and the brain power to pick a winner that wasn't always a bad thing. But then he started pickling what brain cells he had in whisky and any trace of expertise he had went out the window.'

It was like hearing the words inside her own thoughts being spoken aloud, but in Raoul's deep, accented voice they sounded so much worse, so much more appalling that way.

But she hadn't spoken those words. Raoul himself had supplied them to fill the silence. There had been no surprise in his voice; he'd just listed every detail. He had known without being told. He had known everything before he had even arrived here.

So was that why he had come? He'd said there was a scheme that he'd agreed on with her father—to breed horses from his precious stallion. But to do that he would have had to co-operate with Adnan who after their marriage would have been the owner of Blacklands as well as his own grandfather's stud. And who would have owned the magnificent Blackjack.

If the marriage had taken place.

Was that what Raoul had planned? To make sure Adnan didn't marry her and then take over Blacklands?

Shifting awkwardly on the bed, she turned so she could look into the room. The beautiful white lace dress she was supposed to have worn today still hung from the edge of the wardrobe. In the gathering dusk of the evening it looked like a long white shroud, a ghost of what might have been.

'So Adnan was going to come to your rescue—financially?'

She'd heard that cruel note in his voice before. When he'd turned on her, accusing her of being nothing but a gold-digger, only wanting him for his money. That was why she knew what was going through his head now. He was seeing her following the same path with Adnan, marrying the other man only for what he brought to her. In a way it was true, and the only thing she could do was to nod in silent agreement.

She couldn't see Raoul's face but she heard the swift, roughly indrawn breath that revealed his response to her answer. Disgust? Or dark fury? Or just the fact that, deep down, he had always believed this would be the case? To one side, she could see the way his long, powerful fingers clenched over the bedcovers, his bronzed tan dark against the gold and white cotton. The way the material crumpled and bunched damagingly made her stomach clench in instinctive response.

'What I don't understand was what Al Makthabi got out of this.'

Adnan had come to her rescue, put forward the plan of the marriage of convenience, but she had known there had been nothing of the heart in their arrangement. He had promised his grandfather two things—a Derby winner and an heir, and she would help him provide both. The big, black stallion that was the one thing the stud had left of any value was to have been her wedding gift to her new husband, and the heir…

'What did you offer him?' Raoul flung the question at her, cold and sharp.

He was going to hate her answer; hate *her*. Flinching inside at the thought, Imogen pulled the sheets up around her.

'A marriage.'

'Hell, yes, I know there was to be a marriage but—did you sleep with Adnan before you were to take your vows?'

The question burned on his tongue. Of course she had been to bed with Adnan. How could any man have a relationship—an *engagement*—with Imogen and not want—need—to take her to bed?

He couldn't imagine it could be any other way. But, after the heat and passion they had just shared, he could barely control the internal fury and disbelief that raged through him at the thought of her with another man.

'None of your business.'

She was absolutely right. It was none of his business. Or, rather, it had been none of his business. It shouldn't have mattered. But right now it mattered like hell.

'And if you want to know what I…what Adnan was going to get out of this bargain…'

Her voice sounded weird. It was going up and down, swinging all over the place. Was she crying? Or angry? Her face was still turned away from him, her eyes fixed on the opposite side of the room. On that damned wedding dress that was hanging on the wardrobe.

The sight of that damned dress now seemed to have developed the power to stab at him, right in the heart, twisting dangerously in his already uncomfortable conscience.

He had come here to stop the wedding. He had planned to tell Al Makthabi what she was really like. That she was only after him for his money. But when he had met her husband-to-be, he had soon realised that Adnan was nobody's sort of a fool. And that the other man knew exactly what he was getting in Imogen O'Sullivan. The neighbours, the locals who lived in the village, regarded the two families—the O'Sullivans and the Al Makthabis—as the modern day equivalent of lords of the manor. They might believe in the fairy-tale love story of the two big houses joined together, but he knew more about them than that.

He'd told himself that if he'd seen one trace of love in Imogen's face, one hint of that fairy-tale being true, then he would have turned and walked away. But he'd been all sorts of a fool to imagine he might see such a thing. He'd read the signs in her face, the look that said this wasn't a wedding of love, with a bride so happy it shone out of her eyes. And what he had seen in Adnan's face had not been love either.

But even before that had really sunk in, he'd known that whatever happened he couldn't turn and walk away. Couldn't leave Imogen behind and go back to the disturbing emptiness of the past few years when nothing and no woman had satisfied him.

After tonight he knew why. After tonight he

knew that no one could ever make him feel as this woman did. No other woman could make him burn and hunger, the heat of need sizzling up every nerve and leaving him just a husk of a man.

'He got to make his grandfather happy.'

'Quoi?'

He had to drag his thoughts back from the burning paths they'd followed, forcing his mind to focus on what she'd said.

She'd shifted on the bed now, turning back towards him. Although she still held the sheet tucked tight around her, it did nothing at all to hide the sexy enticement of her body. If anything, it made matters worse, with the fine cotton stretched tight over the curves of her breasts. He could clearly see the darker pink of her nipples, the lift of the peaked tips pressed against their covering, and at her hips the fall of the delicate fabric was not enough to hide the shadow of dark hair at the juncture of her thighs. Even just to think of the way he had been buried in her body at exactly that point, with the warmth and moisture of her welcome enclosing him, had his penis stiffening in such a rush that he had to grab the sheets himself and pull them up over the heated evidence of the way he was incapable of controlling himself where she was concerned.

'No need to be embarrassed.' Imogen had seen his reaction and her soft voice, her faint smile, had even more of a damning effect on him.

'Je n'ais pas honte,' he growled, glaring a fierce rejection of her words straight into her face.

He wasn't in the least bit embarrassed by the force of his reaction. It was what had brought them into this bed tonight after all. And it was a response that she shared totally. He'd felt her reaction to his touch, known the way her body melted under his, her spine arching up to press her softness against his chest, his thighs, his pelvis. He'd heard her soft cries of delight and the way they'd morphed into moans of hungry demand as their bodies moved faster and faster, coming together in one mind-blowing, overwhelming rush of release that had had them both collapsing back exhausted on the pillows, their breath coming in great heaving gasps.

He knew what he wanted from this woman and

she knew what she wanted from him. But that was not enough.

Hell, no! He was not going down that path again. Not until he had some things sorted out. He had no doubt about his physical reaction to Imogen—and hers to him—but he'd been that way before and had burned with regret as a result.

'Hell!'

It escaped him at the realisation that the hungry passion he'd felt for Imogen had had him in bed with her—*inside* her—without a pause for thought or even the idea of protection. He had brought condoms with him, damn it; he should have used them.

He'd made this mistake once before, in the out-of-control early days of their relationship. One mistake when desire had overwhelmed him in the warm darkness of the night, on the cliffs above Porto, when he'd had no protection with him, no thought of being able to hold back. Every other time he'd been scrupulous about using contraception but stupidly, irresponsibly, he'd made that one mistake. And one mistake had been all it had taken…

The thought that he might have impregnated Imogen with *another* child of his when she hadn't even cared enough to keep the first one sent black waves of horror crashing through his mind. How had he let the overpowering lust he felt for this woman scramble what little was left of his rational brain cells? He had been thinking only with his.

He hadn't been *thinking* at all!

The realisation pushed him out of bed as if he had been stung. His clothing was still scattered about the floor, evidence if he needed it of how uncontrolled his thoughts had been as they'd made their way up here, tumbled onto that bed…

'What is it?'

Imogen had swivelled round, the sheets twisting even tighter about her. Her face had lost the flush that orgasm had left on her cheeks but there was still that wide-eyed, unfocused look she had turned on him, revealing that, like him, she still hadn't fully collected her thoughts.

'I asked, did you sleep with Adnan?'

He was dragging on his trousers as he spoke.

'You asked me that,' Imogen acknowledged,

her thoughts reeling, remembering the way he had declared he was not ashamed of his growing erection. Not concerned to show that he wanted her again even after so short a time. And she had seen no reason for shame either. In fact, the truth was she had found it a thrill to know that the burning connection between them was still there. That, like the way it had been on those passionate nights in Corsica, he had not been satisfied easily, or quickly, but wanted her again straight afterwards.

So how had they got from there to this in what seemed the blink of an eye?

'And I said it was none of your business.'

'It is my business, seeing as we've just come together—without protection.'

Oh, hell.

She felt as if the whole room had suddenly started to close in on her, growing darker with every breath she sucked in. Raoul's face was shaded and hidden, the brilliant bronze eyes just glittering cold pools above the slash of high carved cheekbones, his mouth nothing but a thin, hard line. What had happened to those softly sensual lips, the hotly demanding mouth that had taken hers so passionately, forcing her own lips open, tongue plunging into her mouth, tasting her, taking her?

Realisation had happened. She could read the thoughts that were going through his mind as clearly as if they were transmitted on to the bleak, withdrawn face.

He had realised what they'd just done; how foolishly they'd behaved. And now, because he so obviously had second thoughts, the horrifying truth dawned on her too.

'You don't need to worry!'

'No?' One black eyebrow lifted sharply, cynically questioning. 'And why not?'

She felt the truth bubbling up like lava in her mouth, but she didn't dare to let it out. Not now, not ever, possibly, as she was sure there was no way he'd ever have wanted to know the truth about the tiny legacy their past relationship had left with her. The heavy sensation of tears clogging the back of her throat told her there was no way she was going to be capable of revealing that truth to him.

So she stuck to the one fact she was sure of, the simple, irrefutable declaration she could make.

'Adnan and I…we haven't, we never, slept together.'

'You've not been intimate?'

It was such a strange, old-fashioned way of expressing it—coming from the man who looked like a bandit, standing there before her with his bare feet splayed out on the shabby bedside rug, dark jeans pulled on roughly so that they were up around his waist but not fully fastened, the belt undone and hanging loose at his narrow hips. His bronzed, broad chest was still exposed, almost shockingly dark against the white and gold décor of her room.

'No—never.' It was vital that he believe her. 'I—I haven't been with anyone at all, not since you.'

'No one?'

His breath hissed in between his teeth and he seemed to come back to himself as if from a long way away.

'But we should have used contraception. And we were damned stupid not to.'

If there was any reason why she could never, ever risk telling him about the child they'd created, the baby she'd lost, then it was there, stamped on his face, dark, brutal and like a mask. The thought that they might have created a child appalled him, horrified him. He would do anything to avoid the possibility.

She couldn't tell him, and she had to reassure him now. She also had to protect herself. It would destroy her to let him express so openly how much he hated the idea of fathering a child with her.

'That…that…will be fine.'

'No repercussions?' It was a lash of a demand, making her skin shiver where the words seemed to land.

'None.'

'Dieu, merci.'

If Imogen had had any tiny trace of hope left then it evaporated at that fervent murmur. The whole atmosphere of passion and hunger that had filled the room only moments before dissolved and vanished, leaving her feeling as flat and limp as the remnant of the sheet that was hanging from her bed. Unable to speak another word, she dragged herself towards her clothing lying on the floor, stooping to pick it up, and then just stood there, tee-shirt and jeans in her hands, unable to do anything more. She couldn't do as he had done and pull on clothes, as if declaring this time was finished. Over and done with.

She knew that was how it should be. There was nothing left between them. The inferno of passion that had consumed them had burned itself out, and what was there to put in its place?

Nothing, Imogen admitted as she watched Raoul's hands go to his shirt to tuck it in at his waist, bringing the belt tight and buckling it with firm, decisive movements. What she might have thought of—dreamed of—as being a new beginning was in fact the end. One final, last sensual fling. A moment of self-indulgence on his part, a wish for oblivion on hers.

But the bill always came in the end.

She had hoped for that insensibility until the morning, one night at least with Raoul by her side, his arms around her, keeping everything that assailed her at bay for just these few hours.

Instead, the brief, bittersweet moments of passion were all she'd had; and the reality she woke up to now was worse than ever before. She had loved Raoul, but he had tossed her aside and walked away from her. She had fought hard to win herself a sort of peace, an acceptance, even after the loss of her baby, and she had thought she'd reached it. She had even let herself think of marriage to Adnan, imagining the brutal wounds Raoul had inflicted had started to heal.

But in just a few days—not even a week—his reappearance and all that followed from it had ripped away the flimsy sticking plaster that she had put over those wounds, opening up the barely closed scars. She was right back where she had started—but this time it was worse. This time she knew the rescue package she and Adnan had offered each other had been blasted to smithereens with no hope of repair. She'd ruined Adnan's life and her own in one blow. Her father's future held only bankruptcy, repossession of the stud, and he would probably now face the bottom of far too many bottles to count.

It would mean she would lose the only home

she'd ever known, her dream of having her family live here, with Ciara finding a base here too, in ashes. All the beautiful horses would be taken in payment of their debts and sent heaven alone knew where. But, worst of all, she would have to face that bleak and empty future knowing she had never truly managed to recover from the love she had felt for Raoul. She still loved him, would probably love him until the day she died, while he had only wanted her to sate the sexual passion he had felt, and she had been weak enough to give into it.

Now it seemed he had had what he'd wanted and, thankful that there would be no possible consequences from this night of passion, he was dressing and on his way. Somehow, she had to find the strength to stand and watch him walk away from her once again.

'Imogen.' Raoul's tone was rough and hard, no sign of any of the softening she might hope for in it. 'This was a mistake.'

'I know,' she managed, waving a hand dismissively in front of her face so she didn't have to look into his. 'But it's fine. No consequences, no ties. We both had…' her voice hiccupped on the word '…fun, and that was that. Now, if you'll excuse me, I need a shower. And you…'

She didn't need to finish the sentence. She was sure the pointed way she glanced towards the door did that for her.

On her way to the bathroom, still with the sheet trailing behind her, she passed the case with the clothes she had packed for her honeymoon. Unable to bear the thought of putting back on the clothes that Raoul had torn from her so ardently, she dropped them on to the floor and snatched up the first items from the top of the case to take them with her into the *en suite.* Turning on the shower with a force that had the water pouring down, she didn't even wait for it to warm up before she stood underneath the torrent, letting it pound down on top of her head. The force of it deafened her ears and numbed her thoughts, bringing on a much-needed state of oblivion.

CHAPTER ELEVEN

SHE WANTED A SHOWER.

Raoul could only stand and stare at the door that Imogen had so forcefully shut behind her. The sound of the shower running seemed like a physical barrier she'd erected between them, cutting her off from him as effectively as the solid wood of the door. Whatever else he'd expected, it had not been that. She wanted to wash away every trace of his touch, his kiss, his possession. It made him feel terrible, vile and *dirty*. As if he had tainted her, when all the time he had…

He had what? It slapped him hard in the face, shaking up his thought processes, leaving him blinking in confusion and shock.

He had wanted to comfort her.

Comfort? How could he feel that towards the woman who had destroyed his child? And how could he be fool enough to have made love to her without any form of protection—no matter how much she assured him that all would be well? How could he risk fathering another child with her when he had no confidence that it wouldn't meet the same fate?

No. That was never going to happen, and there was one way he could make sure of it. The memory of the way she had looked walking across the room, the sheet trailing behind her like the train of a wedding dress, was all the confirmation he needed.

He was standing beside the window, watching the first faint glimmers of the dawn touch the sky, when the sound of the shower ceased. A few minutes later the bathroom door opened and Imogen came back into the room. Her dark hair was wrapped up in a towel turban-style on the top of her head, her feet were bare and she wore a turquoise and white dress that reminded him of the one she had been wearing on that first day on Corsica where he had glimpsed her across the bar and had never been able to look away again.

'You're still here!'

It was obvious that didn't please her. Her voice was tart and her brows drew together in a frown.

'I told you I was never very good at taking orders.'

'I didn't order…'

'You think not? So what was that deliberate stare, the nod of the head towards the door?'

She plonked herself down on the bed, tugging the towel loose and rubbing at her wet hair.

'I thought you'd want to go—you got what you wanted. And, as you said, it was fun.'

'You were the one who said that,' he pointed out. 'I didn't even agree with you.'

The hands that were rubbing at her hair stilled, and he could see she was looking up at him, peering through the black strands.

'Don't lie to me, Raoul!'

'Why should it be a lie? I can assure you that, for me, it wasn't fun.'

So how did she take that? Imogen asked herself, thankful for the concealing curtain of hair that hid the confusion and pain she knew must show in her face. He sounded so serious, her heart twisted in apprehension.

'Just a one-night stand…' she tried and felt the constriction in her chest tighten as she saw that proud dark head move in adamant denial.

Turning, he gestured to where the beautiful lace dress hung from the top of the wardrobe, shrouded in its cotton covering.

'You would have looked beautiful in that.'

'Oh, don't!'

She didn't even want to think about it.

'You still could,' he went on, keeping up that casual, conversational tone. The one that contradicted so starkly the words he was actually saying.

'We should give you another chance to wear it.'

That hit home so hard it knocked her flat, falling back against the pillows, her eyes closing in shock. She had to be dreaming or hallucinating; this couldn't be happening! But when she opened them he was still there, still looking down at her with that skin-scouring stare that seemed to have scraped away a much-needed protective layer, leaving herself raw and vulnerable.

'Better not let it go to waste.'

'Why?' She could barely form the word and it came out in a raw croak. *'How?'*

He couldn't mean what it sounded like, and yet there was no hint of any amusement or anything that might indicate he was anything but deadly serious. With the emphasis on deadly.

'You could always marry me.'

He'd said that before, in the middle of the night, but she'd taken it as a joke. A black, sick sort of joke that she hadn't even let register in her mind. But now he was saying it again and the dark emphasis left her in no doubt that he meant what he was saying.

'But why?'

'Let me see...'

He lifted a hand, ticking off the points he made one by one.

'You need someone to get you out of the financial mess you're in—I can manage that and more. I want the stud. I like what I've seen of it so far—though it needs huge investment and modernisation. I want that stallion Blackjack.'

Didn't he hear what he was saying? Didn't he realise that what he was offering was the reason why he had originally turned away from her so callously?

'But this is what you accused me of before—of wanting you for your money. Like the others, no?' she questioned as he shook his head almost savagely.

'Alice—the others—played a role. They claimed they wanted me for myself.'

'Which is why you pretended you were just a farmer?'

'Until Rosalie told you the truth.'

'That you actually owned the farm and the business. Yes, she pointed out the olive oil in the shops…' Her words dried as she saw the quick frown, the disbelieving look, he had turned on her.

'What else?' he demanded.

'Nothing else! Are you telling me your friend embroidered the truth a little—more than a little—when she reported to you? Did she claim she told me about the worldwide market for your oil?'

Rosalie hadn't needed to add any such thing, Imogen admitted to herself. Because the truth was that she hadn't actually listened—or cared.

If Raoul was just a farmer, or something more, it didn't matter. What mattered was that she had fallen crazily in love with him and all she wanted was for the magical island interlude to carry on into a much longer future. So she hadn't even thought of it, and instead had blundered in with her naïve and over-enthusiastic attempt to persuade him to let their relationship become something so much more than a holiday fling.

'And perhaps she added in the details of the horse breeding programme you were working on? The beautiful stallions I might want to use in the Blacklands stud, just to make sure I bit?'

The answer was written on his face and she almost laughed as she put a hand up to touch his cheek, trace the line of the wry twist to his mouth.

'Believe me, that was more likely to make me want to turn and run, rather than fight my way through your obvious defences. Oh, Raoul, don't you think that perhaps your "friend" was a little interested in you herself? I feel sorry for you,' she added as she saw his eyes change, darkening as realisation set in. 'No—really, truly, I do. If you can't trust anyone.'

'I did once.'

It was a low, muttered growl and the fact that his eyes slid away from hers as he said it told her this was something important. Something he found it hard to speak of.

'I was young, foolish, barely twenty. I met a girl and fell—hard. I thought she had too.'

'What happened?'

'She believed I had money—but it was my father who held the purse strings then. When she found out, she made a play for him instead.'

'She dumped you for your own father?' Imogen couldn't disguise the shock she felt—and her horror—at his story.

'After that I developed a sort of sixth sense where women were concerned. If they wanted money, there were plenty of other places they could find it.'

He made it sound as if it didn't matter, as if he had just tossed those feelings aside. But there was so much control in his voice, in his expression, that Imogen knew he was concealing the full truth.

'I only ever came close to making that mistake one other time.'

'And then?'

His smile was hard, cold, a flash on and off, and then it was gone again, leaving his eyes like polished stone.

'I don't put my head in the noose a second time.'

Imogen flinched away from the cold darkness of the declaration. It echoed back through the years, taking her to a Corsican beach, the slow wash of the waves against the shore in her ears, the warmth of the sun on her back.

'But—isn't that what you're doing now?'

She cursed herself for actually saying it. But she had to. After the way he'd opened up to her, she couldn't just leave things as they were.

'It will be. You're giving me money—paying my family's debts—that's the inducement you're using to get me to marry you.'

She was looking up into his eyes as she spoke and she saw the tiny movement as his head went back, the long, slow blink as he accepted what she had said.

'But this time you're not asking for it. I'm offering it to you. If it means I get you in my bed, then that's a deal I'm prepared to agree to. And I want you, Imogen. More than I've ever wanted any other woman in my life.'

'I don't want…'

A blazing flash from those molten bronze eyes shrivelled the rest of the sentence on her tongue and made it die there unspoken.

'Surely we're past the time for lies? At least we know we're compatible in bed, if nowhere else.'

His words threatened to choke off her breathing. If only he knew how much she wanted to be with him anywhere and everywhere—in bed, out of it; at home or away; *in her life*!

'There's more to marriage than sex.'

Raoul nodded slowly, though his eyes refuted her claim.

'But it's a good place to start—a very good place in our case.'

Unable to stay on the bed any longer, Imogen

pushed herself upwards onto her feet so she could face him, eye to eye.

'You think that because you're hot in bed… Yes, I'm acknowledging that!' she admitted as she saw the quirk of his arched brow. 'I'd be a fool to deny it. But if you think I'd do that—for you…'

'No.' Another shrug. 'Not for me. For your family, your father, the stud, the horses. You could even make sure that Adnan can save face.'

'Oh, come on!'

How could she ever make it up to Adnan? How could he ever forgive her, or at the very least still tolerate her presence in his life? She might as well have renounced him to his face in public. Or turned and walked away from him at the altar.

'How on earth could I do that?'

Raoul looked totally unmoved by her vehemence. Reaching out, he took her hand, lifted it between them, and the smile that slowly curved his beautiful mouth made a trickle of ice slither down her spine.

'We were lovers,' he said smoothly. So smoothly that she couldn't interrupt him, no matter how she might want to refute his words. He had never been her lover, except in the physical sense. 'Long lost lovers who had never forgotten each other, still cared for each other. Still lov—'

'No!' That was too much. How could he even use the word 'love' after all that had gone on?

'Yes!'

He tightened his grip on her hand when she would have jerked away.

'That is the only way it will work—for Adnan's sake. Damn it, woman, you were prepared to marry him; you would have taken everything he was offering—surely you can do this for him now.'

Imogen wanted to deny what Raoul was saying. But she knew she couldn't do any such thing. She couldn't even refute what he was accusing her of doing, though not in the way he meant it. He made her pact with Adnan sound dark and materialistic. A greedy contract based on money and profit only. He knew nothing about the way her ex-fiancé had felt about his grandfather, the way she had wanted to help him fulfil the old man's dreams.

Nor did he know anything about the broken heart that had driven her into that agreement with the man who had once been her best friend. And he never would.

'This way, he'll be a man of honour, doing what was right. He'll be seen as standing aside to let two soul mates—'

'Soul mates!' The words choked her, burning in her throat. 'Never! We're whatever the opposite is…'

She couldn't finish the sentence in the face of his slow nod, the sardonic twist to his mouth.

'*You* might know that—*we* might know that—but for this to work the world has to believe in those soul mates. And so does Adnan. For the devil's sake, Imogen—give the man back his honour.'

So he acknowledged that Adnan had gone into this for honourable reasons—but not her? Of course not; he believed that all she was after was the money—just as he'd decided that had been her motive with him. But at least this way she could give something back to her friend, for what he had been prepared to do to help her. She owed him that at least.

And maybe that way Ciara too would no longer be so angry at what she obviously now saw as a dark lie she found so hard to forgive. Something tugged at her brain, a thought of Ciara meeting Adnan. Worried about the story she had had to spin to her sister, was it possible that she had failed to interpret their feelings for each other properly? But now, if Adnan was free…

'All right. If that's the way you want to spin it.'

It wasn't so terribly far from the truth, was it? She had fallen madly in love with Raoul when she had first met him. She'd been carrying a torch for that love for years. She might have thought her love for him had been lost when their baby had died, but the truth was that she had never truly let go of it. She had always had the tiny, secret hope that if she had gone back to Corsica and found him, if she had told him about the baby they had created between them, then he would at least have given her a hearing. She'd even allowed herself to dream that one day he might realise she had not been after his money but had loved him with all her heart. She still did, she acknowledged miserably, while all the time the dark, sombre sound of the death knell for her hopes and dreams rang inside her heart.

'You call it a spin?' Raoul had the nerve to look surprised, even a trifle shocked. The man could lie through his teeth and not turn a hair, it seemed. 'It's a win-win situation—surely you can see that?'

Win-win for everyone but her. She could marry Raoul and give him what he wanted, give everyone what they needed—rescue her father, the stud, Adnan, even Ciara. At the very least, her sister would have the family home to stay in—and perhaps a chance with the man her sister had once admitted she'd fallen for since she'd come to Ireland, even if she was determined to keep his name a secret. But she couldn't do a thing for herself.

Except to admit to the weakness of dreading watching Raoul walk away from her again as he had done years ago. She didn't know how she'd survived that separation then, and he had only to reappear in her life for her to realise she couldn't go through it again. If she agreed to his proposal—such as it was—then she could at least give herself the double-edged pleasure of knowing she could live as Raoul's wife, loving him with all her heart. But at the same time, she would have to know that he did not love her and had only married her for the business deal he had cold-bloodedly offered her.

But what other choice did she have? He could ruin everyone, destroy them completely, and still walk away from her. Or she could take the little he was offering and pray that one day she might find a way to make him see how she felt—perhaps even bring him to care for her just a little.

Perhaps one day she could end up loving his child, as she had so longed to do years before.

He admitted that he wanted her more than any other woman in the world. Was that enough for her to face the future that lay before her?

It would have to be.

'OK, then.' She forced herself to say it. 'That's the way it will be.'

Raoul's smile was fast and hard, a mere curl of his lips, bringing no light to his eyes at all.

'I knew you'd see sense.'

He was drawing her towards him as he spoke. No force, but he didn't need force—just a gentle, persistent pull that seemed to make her feet move without her volition, her eyes fill with him, her face lift to his for the kiss she knew was coming. The kiss she wanted. So much. If this was all he had to offer her of himself, then she would take it.

The alternative was nothing at all.

'And what would you get out of it?'

Why couldn't she keep her mouth shut? Why did she have to ask the sort of question that could only land her in even more trouble? She knew what he wanted—*all* he wanted—from her. Why did she have to push him to state it bluntly?

'I told you—I get you. In my bed.'

His head had bent and his mouth was trailing hot kisses all over her face, down the side of her cheek, heading for her mouth. Immediately, all the blood rushed to the surface of her skin, waking every nerve, making her shiver and ache deep inside for the heat of his touch, the demand of his possession. She was swimming on a hot sea of need, finding thought impossible, knowing only the hunger he aroused in her simply by existing.

'Is—is that enough?'

His response was a raw, shaken laughter against the side of her throat, hot breath feathering across the hollow where her pulse beat hard and rapid in response.

'Oh, *ma belle*, what do you think?'

His hands skimmed her body, lingering at the curves of her breasts and hips. His teeth took hold of one of the narrow straps of her sundress, tugging it to the side, away and down her arm.

'But it…'

Was she questioning him or herself? This was what he was offering her. *All* he was offering. But was it enough for a lifetime?

'Damn it, Imogen, stop arguing.' It was a rough mutter against her skin. 'If I say it's enough, then it's enough. After all, Adnan was prepared to go ahead for no more.'

'Adnan…'

Could he feel her tension, the shock that ricocheted through her? Could he read her panic, the way her mind reeled away from letting him know the truth?

'He…'

'He what? What the hell else were you offering Adnan as your husband?'

Raoul's tongue slid over the skin he had exposed, tracing an erotic path over the exposed tops of her breasts, making her sigh in swooning response. She didn't want to talk, she just wanted to give in to the molten sensations that were flooding her body, swamping her brain.

'Adnan wanted an heir…' It escaped without thought, without rational control. 'I promised him an heir.'

The shockwave of his reaction was like an atomic explosion close at hand, rocking her sense of reality. He froze, not even breathing against her neck. His very stillness was so terrifying that she was sent scrabbling through her thoughts, trying to work out what she had said.

It burst on her like an ice shower, cascading over her heated skin and taking all the warmth from it in the space between one heartbeat and the next.

'You promised…?'

Raoul's voice wouldn't work. His throat seemed to have been scratched raw so that words would have to force their way past the scars that filled it. He couldn't swallow, couldn't breathe, couldn't think. All that was inside his head was a white-hot roar of fury, one that was slowly turning to ice as it slid through his veins, freezing his heart.

'An heir.'

At least, that was the way it was supposed to sound. But the way he had to force it out tangled the words up, his accent turning them into something that even he couldn't quite make out. The way Imogen turned, as if to question him, was like a bullet right between the eyes. He couldn't repeat the words; couldn't believe what he was hearing. And yet, deep down, he realised he had known all along. Wasn't this what had brought him here in the first place? An instinctive, unconscious awareness of the only reason why Adnan Al Makthabi would marry at all?

He had wanted to stop the wedding, but he had told himself it was because he couldn't stand by and watch as Imogen got her gold-digging claws into another man. But Adnan was no fool. So why would he have wanted to do it? What could

Imogen have promised him in order to win his support?

An heir.

A child.

What else could be worth all that Al Makthabi would have to pay out?

'Raoul…?'

The distance in his withdrawal had communicated itself to Imogen. She knew the reason for it too, if the dawning horror in her eyes was anything to go by.

'Raoul…' she began, her voice in the same condition as his had been.

This was where it began. This was how she was preparing to tell him the truth. She was going to admit what had happened to the child she hadn't even given him a chance to know.

He didn't want to hear it. He didn't want her actually to speak the words.

'No!'

It was sharp, brutal, meant to cut off this topic before it had time to form. He didn't want her to confirm the one thing that could come between them. He wanted to stop this right now, freeze the moment so it couldn't go any further. Before he said something he totally regretted.

'Raoul—we have to talk.'

Imogen felt like she was fighting her way through frozen fog, so thick she couldn't even see Raoul's face, in spite of the fact he was so close. But the ice she took in with each breath told her that he was there and that he had changed from the second she had said that one word.

An *heir*.

'Nothing to talk about.'

Something of the mist had thinned so she could see his expression, and deep down she wished that she'd stayed frozen and blind. There was nothing to help her in the opaque blankness of his eyes, the way his mouth was clamped tight into a thin, hard line.

'Of course there is.'

The shake of his head was adamant, but far worse was the way that he had turned from her, snatching up the shoes that had been discarded on the floor—a lifetime ago, it seemed—and pulling them on with brutal efficiency, his silence shocking after all that had been between them.

What had happened to the ardent, passionate lover? The man who had taken her to the stars and held her as she splintered into a thousand tiny pieces under him? Where was the man who, however unemotionally, had said they should marry?

Did that 'proposal' still hold now? Was she a fool to fear that what she'd said changed everything? That Raoul had no intention of marrying her, even in the businesslike way he had suggested?

He was fully dressed now, shirt buttoned up with frightening precision, belt tightened around his narrow waist. But it was not the clothing or the move away from her that emphasised the distance between them. That was stamped onto his face, etched around his nose and eyes.

'I understand,' she managed. 'If…if you don't want a child.'

Now what had she done to bring his head up like that, the blaze of his eyes threatening to shrivel her where she stood?

'Not want a child?' It hissed in between clenched teeth. 'Of course I want a child.'

Was it relief or lack of understanding that made

her head swim? Or was it the unravelling of bitter memories twisting out from under the mental rocks she had tried to pile on top of them, demanding to be heard?

'I want *my* child.'

It was the tiniest emphasis on that word that told her all she needed to know.

Raoul knew. Somehow he had found out what had happened and he knew all about the secret she had tried to keep hidden. He knew about the baby. Dark tendrils of grief were tangling round her heart, making it impossible to think straight, to find any way to answer him.

'*Our* child,' she hedged.

It did nothing to lighten the glazed darkness in those stunning eyes. There was no easing of the tension in any muscle.

'You can't just demand—'

'Why not?' Dark, brutal, savage. 'You were prepared to have one with Adnan.'

But that had been so much easier. She had cared about Adnan and she would have loved the child. Adnan's child wouldn't have come trailing such memories, complications, such unhappiness and loss. She had known that baby would have been wanted and Adnan would have loved his son or daughter.

'Adnan—Adnan is a friend.'

'We were more than friends.'

'We were not! I fancied you like hell—couldn't keep away from you—but how could we even be friends? I didn't even like you—I still don't!'

Not now. Not when he was this aggressive, this dangerous. How could she like him like this? This was the man who had turned away from her. Who had told her to get out of his life. Who had left her alone with the baby that had never had a chance.

'You would have given Adnan a child. So you would have kept *his* baby if you'd conceived it?'

He was throwing words at her, tossing them at her with such ferocity and speed that they didn't make sense. But there was something else in his voice, a ragged edge to the words that shocked her rigid.

'Would you have kept it for him, or would you have got rid of it like you did mine?'

Got rid? He couldn't think…

'Adnan had promised his grandfather.'

'Don't talk to me about Adnan! This isn't about him—it's about us. About you and me and our child. I wanted that child. I still want it. Our baby. You *owe* me a child!'

CHAPTER TWELVE

HOW LONG HAD the silence dragged on? Was it just minutes since Raoul had thrown those words at her or was it hours?

There was something wrong with her heart. Something wrong with her brain. She couldn't quite absorb the meaning of those hateful words. And yet there was only one possible meaning. Wasn't there?

'You want—' The word swelled up inside her, blocking her throat and choking her.

'The child we should have had.' He sounded no better than she did. 'And when we're married—'

'When we're married? You think I will marry you now—after this?'

Somehow, from deep inside, she'd found a new strength. She didn't know if it came from pain or anger or loss—but she welcomed it as it gave her the courage to speak the truth at last.

'You want me to agree to your terms? You want the stud—and the horses—and a child… Why? You want an heir? Is that it? Why with me?'

'The only person I would ever have wanted a child with was you.'

'Well, that's a pity for you.'

Strength was growing inside her, giving a force to her words that he clearly wasn't expecting. But no, of course he wasn't expecting her to defend herself, to fight back against his accusations. He'd thought she was this callous, careless, selfish creature—for how long? For the two years they'd been apart?

But what did it matter how long? What mattered was what he believed and how wrong he was. And she was going to throw it right in his face and see the truth hit home.

'Because I can't actually guarantee you that child you claim you want. The one you've planned all this payback to bring about. Because, you see, it could be tricky. Adnan knew that but he understood.'

'Understood what?' Raoul demanded when she had paused to gather her strength.

'He understood that it could be a problem because…because it can be difficult to conceive again if you've had…had…'

She lost the words. She could feel the burn of hot tears cascading down her face, taste the salt on them as she had to force her mouth wide open, gasping for the breath that eluded her. Her arms were clasped tight around her middle, holding herself together because she could not afford to fall apart now.

'What? Say the word!'

'Had an ectopic pregnancy.'

He looked as if he'd been slapped hard, right across his face. She could almost see the bruise forming as he blinked, tried to speak, stopped, tried again.

'Ectopic…' was all he managed.

At last she succumbed to the sorrow she had tried to hold back for two long years. The fragile, desperate wall she had built around her memories had crumbled at last and she was lost, head bent, face hidden. She'd held out so long, but she couldn't manage any more. Her legs sagged at the knees, refusing to support her. She was going to fall.

But then arms came around her, warm and powerful. She was supported, held against the hard strength of a masculine chest. She could feel his raw, ragged breathing under her cheek, hear the uneven thunder of a pulse that was as out of control as her own.

'It's all right.'

Raoul's whisper was right next to her ear, the hard pressure of his cheek, the weight of his head on her hair. One hand cupped her face, the other stroked over her skull, soothing her tears.

'It's all right.'

But it would never be all right ever again. Her baby was gone and the fact that Raoul had believed she had got rid of it just made the tears flow faster. She had lost her child—and obviously she had lost its father at the same time. She'd lost him, lost everything.

'It's all right, I've got you. I've got you, Imogen. I'll not let you fall.'

If he said anything else then she couldn't hear it as she abandoned herself to a fury of weeping, unable to hold back any longer. Two years' worth of stored up tears soaked into his shirt, plastering the linen against his skin as she clung onto his arms, feeling the powerful muscles bunch and clench under her fingertips. She swayed against him, felt his long body adjust to take her weight, strong in support.

Then it was as if the world had given way as Raoul's long legs seemed to buckle beneath him. He sank to the floor, taking her with him. Still blinded by tears, by having her face pressed into his shirt, she found herself sitting curled onto his lap, held until the storm of misery gradually slowed, eased, came to a raw, hiccupping stop. Sniffing inelegantly, she managed to lift her head, staring in shock at the mess of black mascara and tear stains marking the white linen.

'I'm sorry,' she said.

'No.' His low, husky assurance sounded worse than she felt. '*I'm* sorry. More sorry than I can ever tell you. I should have known…never have believed…'

But he did believe *her*. That was the one thing that registered. He had never doubted or questioned her declaration that she had lost the baby because it had been an ectopic pregnancy. This couldn't heal the bitter memories—ease the terrible pain, both physical and mental, that she had endured—but it smoothed a balm over the wounds and gave her a new strength. The sort she hadn't known for years.

'I should have trusted… But then I saw that photograph.'

That brought Imogen's head up sharply. She had known the picture of herself and Ciara after their long-awaited reunion had been published in some of the gossip pages, but she had never thought that any of it would be read by Raoul in Corsica.

'It was after… Ciara was helping me.'

'I know.'

If his mouth had been any further from her ear then she would never have caught that low whisper, but it was enough to have her lifting her moisture-smeared face, finding the courage to look into his eyes.

The dampness from her own tears marked his cheeks, running into his rough stubble. Or was it? Blinking to bring him into focus, she could see the moisture that glistened on his thick, black eyelashes, spiking them against eyes that had a suspiciously bright sheen across them.

'Raoul…' At last she had found her voice as she lifted a shaking hand to touch his cheek, his eyes, her heart clenching as her fingers came away wet. 'You believe me?'

'Of course I believe you. You would never lie about something like this. I should have known. And yet when I came—'

He caught, snapping off the sentence as he shook his head. But Imogen needed no further explanation.

'That was when you first came to Ireland?'

A slow, sombre nod of his dark head was his answer.

'I saw you with Adnan.'

Admit it, Raoul told himself, *the jealousy that had burned at the sight of her with the other man—laughing, smiling up into his face—had bitten hard. So hard it had stopped him thinking rationally.*

'I was wrong. So badly wrong. I let the past embitter me. You are no Alice. Or any of the others…'

For a moment, he closed his eyes against the memories. The time he had learned how Alice, tiring of his father's more mature interests, had turned her back on both of them, later aborting the child she had conceived with her new lover in order to live the carefree life with the much younger man.

'I understand.'

'Then you are wrong to.' His voice was rough-edged, dark. 'I don't deserve your understanding.'

With a gentleness that was so much at odds with the grimness of his words, he reached out and wiped the back of his fingers across her cheeks, taking the traces of her tears with them. For one long moment he looked deep into her eyes and a tiny suggestion of a smile played at the corners of his mouth.

'I believed the stories I was told—not once but twice. I believed the worst when I should have believed the best. I came here to ruin your wedding.'

'But that wasn't actually your fault. If Adnan

hadn't come back with Ciara and my father, that scene in your bedroom would never have happened,' Imogen hastened to assure him, but the words had exactly the opposite effect.

'Not the way it happened,' Raoul forced himself to admit. 'But it would have happened. I would have made it happen. I was wrong.'

It was only when he felt Imogen's hand reach up again, one finger outstretched to touch against the corner of his eye and come away with a drop of water resting on its tip, that he knew he had not been able to hide his reactions. But he didn't care. It was what he owed Imogen for the way he'd betrayed her, what he owed the memory of their child that had never had a chance to live. And had almost taken Imogen's life with it.

'But if I can forgive you?' Her voice was soft and so were her eyes, her hand still resting against his cheek, delicate and gentle.

If only she knew what it cost him not to turn his head, to press his lips against her hand. She was warm and soft in his arms, pure temptation, the scent of her skin coiling round him, making his head spin in desire. But that had led him astray before. He could not go down that path again. Not if he wanted to try to appease his conscience and give back to this woman everything he owed her.

'Forgive? *Oh, ma belle...*'

Reluctantly he eased himself into a more comfortable position, pushing his arms underneath her, between their bodies, lifting her from his lap. He felt the cold rush of air like a loss as he moved away from her, taking her upwards, adjusting his stance until he was fully upright, holding her above the bed. He hesitated a long moment, fighting the urge to let his grip tighten round her and draw her close up against his yearning body.

Then at last, unwillingly, he lowered her to the surface of the bed, depositing her softly on the rumpled covers. For a moment, she lay down, her arms still holding him, coming dangerously close to drawing him down alongside her, but he could not let that happen. Putting all the determination he possessed into resisting the demand of his hungry senses, he pulled back and away from her. But he couldn't fight the impulse to drop one last lingering kiss on her upturned face.

'You might be able to forgive, but I cannot. I

can never forgive myself for this. For the damage I have done.'

'But, Raoul!'

Imogen couldn't bear the way that the atmosphere had changed. The moments of empathy, the tears they had shared over the loss of their baby, were evaporating all around them. He was moving further and further away from her with every breath she took and the glaze of sorrow in his eyes was like a warning not to try to bridge the chasm that had opened up between them.

'Non, chérie,' he told her, holding up his hands like a barrier between them as each step backwards took him further away. But the real desperation was what she could read in his face, and that was what kept her frozen in her place, unable to move or to speak. 'I betrayed you.'

'You…'

She wanted to say it but no sound would come. And even if it had she knew he wouldn't listen. So she tried a shake of her head, and saw his slow, dejected smile.

'Oh, yes—not so much here, perhaps.'

One long-fingered hand touched his brow,

pressing just for a moment as if he could wipe away a memory.

'But here.'

That hand flattened hard against his chest, where his heart was. It was the way the pressure of the gesture turned his knuckles white that told her she had lost. She could fight so many things, but not the way Raoul's own conscience was turned against her.

'Let me do this, Imogen,' he said, almost at the door. 'Your future is secure—I promise you that. Whatever you would have gained from our marriage of convenience, it is yours. No strings, no conditions—my gift to you. But let me go. Let me set you free.'

'I…'

Once more she tried to speak, closing her eyes as she forced the words from her numb and unresponsive lips.

'I don't want my freedom—not from you!'

But as she flung the words out, opening her eyes to see the effect they had had, she found she was speaking to the empty air. Raoul had already gone and she was alone.

In an urgent scramble, she pushed herself from the bed and dashed to the door, stumbling over a ragged edge of the carpet as she made her way out into the corridor. The trip and the time needed to recover from it was enough to hold her back for a moment too long. She had barely recovered when she heard the slam of a car door, the roar of an engine.

By the time she got to the front door, all that was visible were the tail lights on Raoul's car disappearing down the drive and out of sight.

CHAPTER THIRTEEN

SO *THIS* WAS where Raoul really lived!

Imogen got out of her car and leaned against the bonnet, staring in total amazement at the wonderful building before her. If she had needed any evidence of the fact that the real Raoul was light years away from the olive farmer she'd thought him, then this was it. Nothing could be further from the simple hotel where they'd shared those passionate nights; the plain inns and restaurants where they'd eaten; the clear blue bays in which they'd swum.

One of those bays, the Gulf of Liscia, stretched out now on the other side of the road, below the steep drop of the cliffs, while behind villa San Francescu the acres of olive trees stretched away into the distance. The villa itself was a fusion of ancient and modern, with the original stonework blended with contemporary touches, like big glass doors to let the sun flood in from all sides.

Over to one side of the sprawling building was a large paddock where several horses, the sturdy bay Corsicans that Raoul bred, contentedly cropped the grass. But Imogen spared the animals only the briefest of glimpses as she made her way across the stone path to rap at the main door.

She had thought she would have some warning of Raoul's approach; that she would see him through the glass in the door or at least catch the sound of his footsteps approaching. But her attention was fixed on the interior of the villa so she missed the silent man who appeared around the corner of the house until he was only inches away from her.

'Imogen.'

The sound of her name spoken in that special way brought her spinning round, her hair flying about her head and catching across her face so she had to tug it away to be able to see properly.

At first he was just a dark silhouette against the brilliant sky, a tall, powerful frame with narrow hips and long, long legs. In a worn black tee-shirt and ragged, cut-off jeans, he appeared much the farmer she had first taken him for, the man she had given her heart to all those years ago. Only the luxury and expanse of his surroundings gave any clue to the power and the wealth that were so much a part of the real Raoul Cardini she now knew. But it was the way her heart leapt and twisted, all in one moment, that left her in no doubt that, whoever he was, whatever his circumstances, Raoul was the man she loved. Totally, without reservation or hesitation.

'Hello, Raoul.'

It was inane, but it was all she could manage. She had spent the length of the journey here thinking and planning, trying to work out just what she would say to him in the moment she saw him; how she would persuade him to listen to why she was here. And how she would convince him that the message she brought was the truth and nothing else.

But one look into his beloved face, one moment of recognition, and every thought fled her mind. All she could manage was, 'Hello, Raoul…' and the hastily swallowed declaration that she was here because she loved him. Because she couldn't be anywhere else and be happy.

'I've missed you.'

Understatement of the year. Was it really only five days since he had walked out of the house at Blacklands, driving away into the cool, pink dawn, heading for the airport and this beautiful villa that was his island home?

Only five days, but he looked as if he had aged in that time. Strain or tiredness…or would she be a fool to hope that the same sort of sorrow and sense of loss that had plagued her had also stolen his sleep at night? He had dark shadows under those spectacular eyes and his hard jaw was shadowed with a growth of stubble that indicated he hadn't taken the time and trouble to shave for a day or more.

'I would have been here earlier but there was an accident.'

'Not you? Your sister?'

The sharpness of his voice gave her room to hope.

'No, not me. And not Ciara either. I still don't

know where she is—or Adnan. She rang me again, just once. Said she and Adnan were fine—but they wanted to be by themselves for a while. I had to promise not to try and find them—or let anyone else do it. No, my father had a fall from Blackjack, and we had to get him to hospital. He broke his leg—but he's doing well now.'

'So why aren't you there with him?'

'He told me to come, and I had to talk to you anyway. We can't go on as things are.'

'We can't? I thought things were exactly as you wanted them.'

There was no warmth in his response, no light in those beautiful eyes. Had she got this all wrong? Had she misread him? The memory of that gesture of his hand from his head to his heart had been playing on a loop inside her thoughts over and over again, ever since the morning he'd declared he couldn't forgive himself.

'It's not how I want things. Look—do we have to do this out here? Couldn't we go inside and talk?'

'Of course.'

Stiff-backed, stiff-faced, he strode past her towards the door, pushing it open and holding it so she could precede him. Was she imagining things or was he holding himself just that little bit too far away, making sure no part of her body touched him as she stepped into the cool, tiled hallway? After the sun outside, the interior seemed dark and she had to stand, blinking, as her eyes adjusted to the change in light. Behind her she heard Raoul come inside too and stand so close that she could feel the warmth of his breath on her neck.

'I've missed you too,' he said, low, rough and totally unexpected.

'What?'

Imogen spun round, her hair swinging out again, catching on the rough stubble on his chin. It was the look in his eyes that caught and held her as his hand went up to free the shiny black strands. It was only when she had to take in a long, deep breath, and then another, that Imogen realised he was taking far too long about it, his fingers lingering, reluctant to let go.

'Raoul…'

His head snapped up, the mouth that had softened, lips parting, clamping tightly shut again.

'I'm forgetting my manners. Would you like a drink? Some coffee—or perhaps water?'

'To hell with your manners!'

She couldn't hold it back and knew from the stunned blink that the force of her response had shocked him.

'That isn't what I came here for!'

'Then why are you here?'

He'd made a mistake with that admission of missing her, Raoul acknowledged to himself. It was stupid and totally inappropriate after the efforts he'd made to free her from the relationship that he'd made such a mess of. But he hadn't been able to hold it back. In the moment that she'd walked past him and he'd caught the soft scent of her skin, mixed with a delicate floral perfume that the warmth of the sun had brought to the surface, he had felt every cell in his body awaken to the intoxication of her presence and the revival of the memories he'd been struggling to put aside. They were the images that had haunted his thoughts, tormented his body, every night as he'd tried to settle to sleep. In the end, he had given in and gone out to the stables, saddled one of the horses and ridden through the darkness of the night until both he and the stallion were slow with tiredness and his eyes were closing even as he headed home.

But, once back inside the house in his bed, even the exhaustion had failed to claim him. He'd lain, staring up at the darkness of the sky, fighting an ugly battle with the images of Imogen as he had last seen her playing across his mind, tormenting his body into further restlessness.

The Imogen who had turned up so unexpectedly at his door could have been the girl he had met two years before. The loose waves of her dark hair gleamed in the sunlight, and the soft cotton of her simple blue dress was so much like the sundresses she had worn before that just for a moment he'd actually let himself think that he was back in that time. Back in the days when their relationship had been new and fresh, and he'd had hopes of a future.

'Imogen, tell me what's brought you here.'

'I came here to bring you this.'

As their words clashed in the air, slowly Raoul realised that Imogen was holding up a briefcase, pushing it towards him as if she wanted him to take it.

'What is it?'

'There's no need to look at it as if it's a snake about to bite you!'

There was a shaken edge of laughter in Imogen's voice.

'It's just paper.'

'Paper?'

He didn't understand or believe that, Imogen knew. It was stamped all over his face. And the way he eyed the briefcase tugged on something in her heart, so she couldn't drag this out any further.

'These came on Monday.'

Snapping open the briefcase, she pulled out the sheaf of papers it contained and waved it in front of him.

'From you.'

Could his eyes look any more blank or his face show any less expression? That was what gave him away to her, telling her without words just how hard he was fighting not to reveal anything.

'Yes. I wanted you to have them.'

Then when she caught her breath in an effort not to break down, to tell him what she really felt, his eyes flashed to her face and she saw the burn of intense emotion flaring in their golden depths.

'I told you I would make everything all right. I promised,' he said.

'You promised.' Slow and careful, it revealed the battle she was having for control of herself. 'You promised—but you didn't ask if it was what I wanted.'

'Imogen, it was what I owed you. What you would have had if you'd married Adnan—what I took from you.'

'No.'

She saw the swift dark frown, the burn of anxiety on his face, and it almost destroyed her. But she'd started on this now; there was no going back. And this was the only way to show him the truth. To show him how she felt.

'No, Raoul, you took nothing from me.'

'I did.' It was raw and ragged, his hand coming up in a gesture of surrender. 'Everything I did was wrong. I ruined your wedding plans, I behaved like a monster and I destroyed the future of the stud—your father's freedom. If you'd married Adnan...'

'But the truth is that I could never—*would* never—have married him,' Imogen admitted, knowing there was no way forward but the truth. 'Even if you hadn't turned up, I could never have gone through with it. I knew that. I was thinking it already in the church, that day you found me. And then when I saw you there—well, nothing was the same after that. I don't know what I would have done, what I could have done, but, once I remembered that you were in the world, how could I ever marry another man?'

'But...' It was just a croak of sound, of disbelief.

'Yes, I know. There was everything Adnan had promised me—and everything I'd promised him. But how could I go through with that? How could I marry him, have his baby, when the only child I ever wanted was the one we made between us? The one that...'

'Oh, mon Dieu!'

Raoul was moving forward, enfolding her in his arms, holding her tightly. The briefcase fell to the floor and the papers she still held were crushed between them.

'Imogen—I wish I'd known.' The thickness of his tone told her of the emotion that clogged his throat, and the rough, unsteady pulse of his heart underneath her cheek revealed the struggle he was having for any degree of composure.

'I wish I had known. I wish I could have done something.'

'There was nothing anyone could have done.' It was barely a whisper, buried in the protective cave of his arms, but she knew he had heard it when she felt the heavy, raw intake of his breath and the sorrowful nod of his head in acknowledgement.

'But I could at least have been there.'

'And how I wish you had been. We both lost so much that day.'

'Because I listened to the wrong person,' Raoul admitted, the words rasping desperately.

'You'd been hurt—badly. I never realised quite how badly until I came here and saw…'

From under his arms her hand waved unsteadily, taking in the luxurious surroundings, the huge estate beyond the glass doors. 'It must be so hard to know whether someone wants you for you—or for…' Her voice sank even lower. 'Or for this.'

Slowly, carefully, she eased from his grasp, lifting her head so she could look into his eyes and meet that questioning gaze head-on.

'That's why I had to bring this back to you.'

Raoul's burning eyes went down to the documents she held. The legal forms that sorted out the whole sorry mess that she and her father had been. Financial provision for the stud, the stallion Blackjack and the small fortune needed to pay her father's debts, and keep them solvent for many years to come.

'I can't take it, Raoul—I don't want it.'

'But how will you manage if you don't? I *wanted* to give it to you. I wanted you to have it. I wanted to try to repay all the wrong that I'd done you. The way I rejected you. It will never be enough…'

'No,' Imogen agreed and she saw the way that shock landed like a blow on his face, bringing his head up high and sharp. 'No, this is not enough, Raoul.' She smiled sadly. 'And it will never be.'

'Then what else do you need? How can I make sure that you're happy going forward? How can I give you everything you need?'

'You can't.'

'But I will. I'll try. Just ask and—' he began, but she reached up a hand to lay it across his mouth, closing his lips, silencing him.

'There isn't enough money in the world to give me everything I need,' she told him, turning her hands so she was holding onto his arms, feeling the warmth of his skin, the strength of powerful muscle even through the papers she still held. 'Because money won't do it. Money can never do that.'

She knew her words had hit home when she felt his total stillness, the tension that held his muscles taut, his long body pressed against hers.

'You don't want…'

It was as if he was exploring his thoughts, and trying to discover hers, finding his way slowly through a mass of confusions; travelling blind, as if he was afraid to find that the truth he'd thought he was aiming for was in fact something entirely different. And it was that hesitancy that made her heart swell with the thought that she'd judged him right and he really understood.

'I don't want anything that money can buy,' she assured him. 'How can that give me everything I need when what I need…'

At this last moment her nerve almost failed her and she had to snatch in a hard, strengthening breath in order to be able to continue.

But when she looked into his face, and saw the beginning of hope start to flare in the depths of his eyes, she knew she'd made the right move, staked all her future on the right hope. The answer to what she needed was right here in front of her.

'You said you wanted to make sure that I'm happy going forward. And the truth is that the only way I can be happy going forward is if you go forward with me.'

'You want me?' It was just a breath.

'I want you.' His faintness made her strong and the declaration was brave and bold, joy spreading along every vein, every nerve, bringing a brilliant, assured smile to her face.

'I want you. And only you. I love you, Raoul. You are my future—the only life I want is with you.'

'And me with you.'

Raoul rubbed a hand across his eyes, blinking hard as he focused on her uplifted, intent face.

'Is it possible? Can we really try again? Begin afresh? Can we have a future?'

Imogen felt her lips curve into the smile that was growing inside her heart.

'Why not try?'

She hadn't even finished speaking before he was down on one knee before her, holding her hand tight, looking up into her face with an expression that spoke of a near-desperate hope, a longing to get this right.

'Imogen, will you do me the real honour of being my beloved wife? For today, tomorrow, our future? Our life?'

'I will. Oh, Raoul, yes, I will—but…'

She'd shocked him now and she saw the hope leave his eyes and darken his face, so she had to hurry to reassure him.

'But I can't promise a baby.'

'Sweetheart…'

He was on his feet in a moment, holding her close.

'My darling—you are the only person I ever want a child with, and if it happens, then I will be the happiest man in the world. But, if it's not to be, then you are still the only woman I want to have as my wife, to go into the future with.'

His lips came down on hers, crushing back all the fears, erasing all the doubts and replacing them with hope and happiness.

'You are my love, my life,' he said when at last he had to lift his head to snatch in a much-needed breath. 'And together we can create a world worth living in.'

'Our world,' Imogen echoed, soft and sure. 'Our world—together.'

* * * * *